SINS & SCIENCE

NATASHA TREMBLAY

Milton, Ontario

Brain Lag Publishing
Milton, Ontario
http://www.brain-lag.com/

Cover design by Catherine Fitzsimmons

Library and Archives Canada Cataloguing in Publication

Title: Sins & science / Natasha Tremblay.
Other titles: Sins and science
Names: Tremblay, Natasha, author.
Identifiers: Canadiana (print) 20210244283 | Canadiana (ebook) 20210244348 | ISBN 9781928011569
  (softcover) | ISBN 9781928011576 (ebook)
Classification: LCC PS8639.R45425 S56 2021 | DDC C813/.6—dc23

Content warnings: Death, graphic injuries, medical procedures, suicide

Trigger warning!

If you are troubled by self-harm and mental illness, blood and gore, virtual worlds and string theory, Catholicism and blasphemy, sexual arson and vows of abstinence, mutant rats and switchblade-wielding children, coconut trees and the North of England, populist Popes and drug-using exorcists, unclean old men and dizygotic twins, failed lawyers and claims-adjusters-turned-bartenders, then this book is not for you.

Should such topics pique your curiosity, please read on, and more importantly, consider consulting a professional.

Sincerely,
Natasha Tremblay

To my mother

If this book is well-received, I wish to thank you for all your help and your unwavering encouragement.

If this book scandalizes its readers, I wish to once again apologize for my impulse-control issues and complete lack of a filter.

CHAPTER ONE

Dalton McGovern could no longer bear the weight of it all. Everyone around him expected nothing short of excellence from him. Having the greatest scientific mind of a generation, however, is of little significance without the strength of character one needs to overcome adversity. And at the age of twenty-eight, the Oxford-educated computer scientist was now taking more of an interest in biology. Indeed, sitting on the kitchen floor of his Liverpool flat, he evaluated that a quick, clean cut, half an inch deep, into his forearm, down to his wrist, would do the trick. The greatest challenge would be to overcome the pain after the first incision and repeat the operation on the other arm. Best to start with his left arm then, as he was left-handed. He deemed he would have a greater chance of succeeding using his dominant hand, despite the injury.

For the past three years, Dalton had felt trapped in a fog of emptiness. Everywhere he went, no matter who he saw, or what he did, he simply felt nothing. When Karl left him, he felt no heartbreak. When he completed his doctorate, he felt no joy. When his mother passed, he felt no sadness. Everything moved in slow motion around him, as though he were disconnected from the real world and caught in a void of apathy. Today, he would finally put an end to his lonesome torment.

Without getting up from the floor, he reached up toward the

kitchen counter, where weeks' worth of dirty dishes was piled. He grabbed a steak knife and pointed it to his arm. For a moment, he hesitated. *You're pathetic. Can't even end your miserable existence,* he thought. *Stop thinking. You always think and never get anything done. For once in your life, fucking do something.*

And Dalton successfully plunged the knife into his arm. It took a split second before he felt pain. The wound was deep, and blood began to pour out as though it were hardly contained inside him to begin with. When the pain hit, Dalton's first instinct was to pull the knife out. But he stayed in control. *Mind over matter. The worst is done. Now, just slide it down to your wrist. Fucking do it already!* Dalton forced the blade down to his wrist, which was harder than he'd imagined. He groaned and forced the knife through the skin, flesh and nerves that stood between him and his objective. An abundance of blood now flowed out of his arm, dripping all over his body and legs, and pouring onto the floor. He watched as his blood travelled between the cracks of the grey tiles, the stream being guided in a contained and orderly fashion as it spread across the kitchen floor. That pleased him.

With great difficulty, he grasped the knife with his left hand to repeat the operation on his right arm. The awful burning sensation that radiated from his wound throughout his entire body was very nearly enough for him to give up. *Fuck the pain. You want it to stop? It will stop once you've finished what you started.* Dalton channelled the energy the pain generated into his left hand, and, in a far less calculated manner than he had with the initial wound, he madly slashed at his right arm over and over until enough blood sprayed and poured out for him to consider the wound sufficiently severe to achieve his goal.

The burn Dalton felt in his arms gave him some final satisfaction before his imminent death. It was the first time in years he had felt something so vividly. At last, he felt real. He felt very much alive, with death just around the corner. And then he felt nothing.

Only darkness and eternal solitude.

*   *   *

Darcy McGovern liked to consider herself a little bit psychic. This trait of hers was particularly strong when it came to her twin brother. All day, she had been overwhelmed with a terribly empty feeling, as though she were trapped in a void of hopeless despair. It was certainly out of character. Darcy always balanced out her gloomy brother with her cheerful personality. Today, however, she *just knew* something terrible was bound to happen. That feeling led her down Glendevon Road until she reached Dalton's terrace home, where she'd been standing outside the door for about a minute, knocking.

"If you don't open up, I'm coming in anyways. I've still got Karl's old key, you know." No answer. In addition to her concern for her brother's well-being, the wind was blowing hard that day and it was bound to rain soon, and Darcy failed to see why she should stand outside any longer. She wiped her feet on the rude welcome mat that she had bought him for their last birthday, staining the words *No need to linger* with the dirt from her shoes. She pushed open the wooden door and the hinges screeched.

A cool draft from the kitchen brought with it a metallic scent all too familiar to Darcy, combined with the stench of rotting food abandoned on the counter. She rushed to the kitchen. On the kitchen floor lay her twin brother, in a pool of his own blood.

"Now, what have you got yourself into this time?" she asked the motionless body. Steady as always, she called for an ambulance, and began to dress his wounds with what she could find—a dishrag, that she soaked in gin. In Afghanistan, Darcy had seen even more rudimentary treatments do the trick. He had lost a lot of blood, but he could still survive. "We all die at some point, but there's no need to rush into it," she advised her unconscious twin.

The ambulance arrived and took Dalton away. Darcy told the uninterested paramedics, "I know he's still with us somewhere. I can *feel* it. I'm a bit psychic, you know."

Indeed, what was left of Dalton's consciousness grasped at the last thread of existence on which it could cling. Like butter spread too thin on a slice of bread, Dalton felt himself slowly fading away.

And then, he woke up.

*   *   *

It is difficult to say whether being a loss adjuster makes a person cynical, or if cynical people are simply drawn to such an occupation. Regardless, Isidora Prentice's belief that people, by nature, were fundamentally self-serving and dishonest made her very good at her job. On that grey Tuesday afternoon, Isidora walked around a burned-down bed and breakfast and was treated to a private theatrical performance starring the owner of the ashy inn. He was seated on the pavement with his feet stretched out onto Bagot street, elbows on knees, head in hands. Isidora pretended to ignore him as she examined the damage within the scorched establishment. However, she found herself entertained by his dramatic monologue.

"My lifelong dream has vanished into ash and flames!" he cried. "Why must God punish me so ruthlessly? I am a good man. A good man, I tell you!"

She couldn't help but join in. "I don't believe God is to blame," said Isidora as she pushed aside some ash from the ground with her foot, hands in the pockets of her red jacket. She looked down, and a thick lock of her blonde hair fell in front of her pale blue eyes. The temperature hovered just above freezing, so she hesitated a moment before taking her ungloved hand out of the warmth of her pocket to pull the stray lock back behind her ear. With her foot, she uncovered a charred object about half an inch wide and a couple inches long. She leaned down and picked it up, flicking the ash off it with her finger and uncovering its metallic top.

"Do you smoke, sir?" The object, though melted and misshapen, was visibly a cigarette lighter.

"Are you offerin' me a ciggy or are you accusin' me of something? I know why you're here and what your type do to honest men like me." The owner stood up and joined Isidora inside the remains of the inn. He hovered behind her, looking over her shoulder at the cigarette lighter.

Isidora's gaze turned from the lighter towards the owner. "I smoke," she said, a half-smile playing on her lips. She pulled a cigarette from a pack in her pocket, placed it in her mouth, flicked the lighter and managed to get a few sparks out of it. The fourth spark was enough to light her cigarette. "Still works."

She looked back at the spot on the ash-covered floor where she'd found the lighter. Just above was a window frame. *Large window, large, flammable curtains,* she thought. *What a dull way to start a fire. He could have at least gone for something a little more explosive!* She looked back at the floor where a few singed fragments of the curtain material lay. She picked up a piece and held it up between her thumb and her index finger at the owner's eye-level. She took the cigarette out of her mouth with her other hand and held it to the material until it ignited. The owner watched as the flame consumed the curtain, slowly.

"Business was going well then, was it?" asked Isidora, looking straight into his eyes. She didn't flinch or blink as the flame reached her finger. She blew it out and he blinked as the smoke stung his eyes.

She looked down. He was digging the nails of his left hand into the palm of his right. *Strange tic. The hands always betray the liar.* Her eyes shifted back up from his hands toward his eyes while she awaited a response.

The owner stuck to his story. "Yes, ma'am." His nails sank deeper into his palm.

"There are better things you could do with your retirement," said Isidora. "Especially with a nice sum from your insurer. I would go to Nice." The owner frowned and his breathing began to accelerate. *Well, he didn't last very long.*

"The bizzies ruled out arson. You're just trying to find a way out of giving what's due to an old man, you cheap bastards!"

"Who said anything about denying your claim?"

The owner's anger got the best of him. "I didn't light the curtains on fire! You're a con artist, and a fraud. You should be ashamed of yourself. How do you live with yourself, ruinin' people who've already lost everything?"

Isidora had little trouble living with herself. Exposing people for what they truly were was quite satisfying to her and getting paid to do so was certainly better than allowing this ability to plague her personal relationships. Determining she had all the information she needed, Isidora left the inn and flagged down a cab.

When it turned the corner to Sandown Road, Isidora swore upon spotting her 10-year-old nephew Stanley Wexler pounding on her glass-panelled front door like an idiot. His bike, of course, was over on its side. *Will the boy ever figure out how to use his kickstand?* she wondered as she got out of the cab.

"Oy! Auntie Izzy! Lemme in! I'm hungry! Auntie Izzy!" Stanley shouted at the closed door. She slammed the cab door shut, and Stanley spun around. The wide grin on his face revealed the many gaps between his teeth. He waved.

"What the bloody hell are you doing here?" asked Isidora. She marched over and inspected the door, discovering several of his greasy handprints on the glass. She took a tissue paper from her purse and began wiping the marks.

"Ma's working overtime again, so I came over," said Stanley as he watched his aunt polish the door.

"Of course she is. Of course you did. Of course she didn't bother texting me and just sent you over. It's not like a single woman in her twenties would have anything better to do, like go on a date. No, of course not. My social life amounts to babysitting me bloody sister's progeny," she said, turning to look him over. "And of course you didn't tie your bloody shoes."

"It's too much trouble, tyin' me shoes just to take 'em off again," said Stanley. Isidora opened the door. He pushed past her, stepped inside, kicked off his sneakers and darted to the kitchen. He sat down at the table. "I'm hungry."

Isidora nearly tripped on one of his shoes as she walked down the hallway toward the kitchen. She microwaved some leftover spaghetti and served it as dinner at the kitchen table, accompanied by some boxed wine for herself.

Stanley picked a dusty silk flower from an arrangement in a vase in the centre of her table, a remnant of a bridesmaid bouquet from five years ago. Isidora kept them on the table because they amused her; the flowers had lasted longer than the marriage. Stanley held the flower under his nose, took a deep whiff, quickly pulled away from it and tossed it on the floor.

"These flowers are no good. They don't smell nice. Ma grows

real zinnias, the nicest in the neighbourhood."

"Of course she does."

"I will bring you some when they bloom."

Isidora shrugged and poured herself a generous glass of wine. "So, Stanley, tell me about school."

"Good," he replied politely.

"Why?"

Stanley wasn't expecting to have to justify his answer. "Well, I've got loads of friends. I'm the fastest runner."

Isidora frowned slightly. "Friends and running hardly relate to school itself. When you're sitting in the classroom, how do you feel?"

Stanley had not thought of it before. But he tried. "Pretty bored, really. And I have to sit next to a nasty girl, Chloe. She thinks she knows everythin', answerin' all the questions."

Isidora considered her nephew's complaints. "Yes, right. After all, the fastest runner in school can't be bested by the girl he fancies... especially when she doesn't return his feelings."

"Fuck off! Ma says you drink too much and that everyone hates you. She says you'll never marry and that you'll die alone, miserable, and you'll rot in Hell, just like me great-aunt Sylvia! And I won't bring you any zinnias, not even to put on your grave."

He stormed out the front door and grabbed his bike. Isidora figured she should probably try and stop him, or at the very least, figure out where he was headed, but considering his poor manners and her sister's alleged opinion of her, she didn't particularly feel like doing anything more for them. She'd already shared what was supposed to be her dinner for the rest of the week.

Sitting alone at her kitchen table, Isidora lit a cigarette and poured herself more wine. *Am I really going to die alone and go to Hell?* She fell asleep at the table, the now empty wine box pillowing her head.

*   *   *

"Enjoyed yer nap?" asked Darcy, who was sitting next to her brother's bed eating hospital pudding. She offered him a spoonful.

"It's butterscotch." He groaned and shook his head in response. He'd only just woken up from his suicide attempt. Nearly dying had cut his appetite.

The hospital lights were far too bright and his sister's voice far too loud. Although he felt light-headed, he attempted to sit up slightly. He looked at his sister, whose large grey eyes still had their humorous glow. She had French-braided her shoulder-length, dark brown hair. He knew she always braided her hair in difficult times. With her hair out of the way, she had one less thing to worry about.

"You lost a lot of blood, which meant *I* had to lose a lot of blood, which also means I get to have some pudding," Darcy said. "Since that's my blood in your veins now, you can't just do whatever you want with it. It's mine, and I'm telling you, you have to take good care of it. No more nasty cuts," she said, pointing her spoon at his bandaged forearms as she spoke those last four words. She finished her pudding.

"I saw death," Dalton said, his voice faint.

Darcy raised her eyebrows. "And? How was it?"

"It was nothing. Absolutely fucking nothing. Just darkness, and loneliness, for all eternity."

Darcy nodded. "Happy to hear it's shit. That means you won't be in a rush to go back."

Dalton sat up quickly, which made him feel even more woozy. The rapid movement also made him aware that his arms hurt.

"Easy, now!" said Darcy.

"That's it!" said Dalton. "My next project. I've got it!"

Darcy's eyes widened.

He continued, "I was out of ideas. Uninspired. Purposeless. Destined to giving lectures to uninterested half-wits."

Darcy's skepticism showed through clearly as she listened to her brother's delusions. "You're on lots of meds, love." Her remark didn't tone down his enthusiasm.

"What if I could create the afterlife?" he said.

Darcy burst into laughter. She always found her brother's God complex as amusing as it was problematic.

"Just get some rest."

Dalton lay back and shut his eyes. Obviously, his stupid sister would never understand his abilities. But as he rested, he brainstormed the answer to life's greatest mystery.

*   *   *

Dalton's recovery progressed well. He was to be released from the hospital in a matter of minutes, now. After being harassed by psychiatrists for days, he finally accepted a prescription for antidepressants he knew he wouldn't need. It seemed a waste to have to throw so much medication down the toilet. But he couldn't let serotonin reuptake inhibitors interfere with his mind, not when he had to work on the most important scientific achievement in the history of mankind. He waited for Darcy to come pick him up. Instead, his ex-boyfriend, Karl Schmidt, showed up.

"What the bloody fuck?" asked Dalton.

Karl smiled gently and said, "Darcy told me you were not feeling very well, and I wanted to check on you."

Dalton glared at him. "Your English is as shit as ever."

Attacking Karl's slight German accent was rather uncalled for. However, Karl did leave him abruptly without any explanation, so a bit of hostility was to be expected.

Karl ignored the attack and offered to drive Dalton home. He had already told Darcy he would be doing so, which left Dalton no choice but to go along with it. As Karl drove, Dalton kept his arms crossed and stared out the window of Karl's Volkswagen Golf. Dalton really wanted to give him the silent treatment, but he had a lot of questions and he felt the silent treatment may have been punishing him more than Karl, who seemed quite at peace keeping his eyes on the road.

"Where were you all this time?" asked Dalton, with only a slight hint of bitterness in his tone. He looked at Karl, who was surprisingly tanned. He had new glasses, too. They were round, with a thick, burgundy frame. Dalton found they detracted from his hazel eyes. He had let his black hair grow out a bit, which gave him a new devil-may-care look that Dalton admittedly found quite attractive. Of course, Karl was still astonishingly thin for a grown man, and he apparently still insisted on wearing jeans with a suit jacket. Today, the jeans were white, the jacket, grey. But something was different about him since the last time Dalton had seen him. He no longer seemed like the overworked young lawyer he had known. Karl was without a doubt far more relaxed.

"I was in Israel for a while."

Dalton laughed. "Ironic."

Karl didn't get it and carried on with his story. "I then travelled to India, before going to Ghana. Finally, I came back to Europe and spent some time in Marseille. Then your sister called me."

Little did Dalton know, Karl had a total burnout after being overworked as a young corporate lawyer in a large firm specializing in insurance law and went on a quest for spiritual enlightenment. He hoped to find it in Jerusalem, but only found boredom upon seeing historical monuments. He hoped to find it in Kashmir, but only found an allergy to ginger. He hoped to find it in Ghana, but only found out the hard way it was possible to get malaria despite getting the recommended immunization. Karl gave up on his spiritual quest, went to Marseille, and realized the negotiating skills he had developed as a lawyer, the French he had learned in school, and the friends he'd made travelling through the Middle East came together nicely. Indeed, Karl became a key player in illegal arms dealings between France and the Maghreb countries. However, he dropped it all when Darcy emailed him about Dalton's suicide attempt.

"Why did you go?" asked Dalton.

Karl paused. "I was looking for something I couldn't find."

Dalton laughed. "You were avoiding your responsibilities, because you couldn't handle it anymore. You weren't looking for anything, you were running away."

Karl took one hand off the wheel and gently touched Dalton's right arm, where several nasty scars had formed. "Just like you."

Dalton watched Karl's index finger slowly trace a long stitch on his right arm. Dalton pulled his arm away. "Unlike you, I came back with answers."

Karl parked the car. "If you'll allow me to come inside, I'd be very interested in hearing your answers, for I am full of questions."

Dalton's pride was telling him to send Karl away, but he felt the urge to reveal to someone his solution to death. He invited Karl inside his home, which was now spotless, thanks to Darcy. Karl took the liberty of preparing some tea for the two of them.

"Oh, sure, make yourself at home again. Come and go as you please!"

Karl sat down and gave Dalton his cup. "Tell me about those answers of yours."

CHAPTER TWO

Quentin Campbell had learned from personal experience that with a good barrister and a thick arresting officer, you can cut your best mate's throat with a broken beer bottle and only go to prison for a few years. The trouble is, afterward, you have to find a new best mate to pick you up from prison, and not many blokes want to be best mates with someone who cut their last best mate's throat. Your new best mate might be an unreliable beaut like Edward Reid, who leaves you waiting five and a half hours outside Liverpool prison until he finally shows up, piss drunk. Though Quentin had built up a great deal of anger waiting for Edward, when he finally showed up in his seventeen-year-old Audi, Quentin felt relieved more than anything as he settled into the passenger seat. Anything to get away from the old man.

"So, how was prison?" asked Edward. He scratched his ginger beard, picked up a can of beer from the cup holder, took a swig, and passed it to Quentin, who finished it.

"Sound," he said. Quentin looked out the window, but night had fallen, and he saw only his own reflection, his dull, brown eyes looking years older than they had when he'd first been locked up.

"Lettin' you finish your sentence early on good be'aviour. Good be'aviour! Never seen you be'ave good in your life," said Edward.

"I just wanted to get away from the bloody ol' man."

"The daft ol' cellmate you was tellin' me about?" Edward laughed gutturally, revealing his striking overbite and large gap between his two front teeth.

"Yeah, remember how the gov'nor kept on jokin' about how lucky I was not to have a cellmate? I mean, I knew the ol' man wasn't all there, but he was bloody clingy." Quentin crushed the beer can with his tattoo-covered hand and tossed it out the window.

"I thought you said he just sat around all day in his bed ramblin' on about some nonsense."

"Yeah, the bloke was ancient. His clobber was proper antwacky. And he kept on complainin' about schoolchildren."

"You're startin' to look pretty ancient yerself, fuckin' greyin' all over, like." Edward tousled Quentin's dark, curly hair aggressively. Quentin pulled away and shoved him back. The car swerved.

"But this fuckin' ol' man took a likin' to me."

"A bloody poof."

"Followed me around everywhere like a bloody dog I'd have to shoot between the eyes."

"What kind of a sick bastard shoots a dog?" Edward's tone instantly changed from amused to stern.

"Even when I thought I'd lost him, he'd be right behind me shoulder, repeatin' the same shit over an' over. 'Bad children must be punished.' Clearly some sort of child murderer."

"Or molester." Edward laughed. "Show me on the doll where the ol' bugger touched you." Quentin shoved Edward again. The car swerved a little more.

"And he smelled like shit, too. Like rotten eggs. I couldn't bloody stand it anymore and asked for a cell transfer. The gov'nor himself came to see me, looked at me like I was mad, said I was lucky and should shut it."

"So you had to keep sleepin' in the same room as your pedophile?"

"I told the gov'nor I couldn't stand the ol' man, that he was always hangin' aroun', pissin' me off, sayin' all this rubbish..."

It looked physically difficult for Quentin to finish telling his story, almost like it pained him; he locked his jaw, shut his eyes and took a deep breath before carrying on. Edward knew Quentin was a hard man who didn't feel pain. Nonetheless, the visible struggle gave Edward a violent chill like someone had tossed a bin of ice water over him.

"Well, go on, then!" said Edward.

"So, as I was explainin' me'self to the gov'nor, I noticed the fuckin' ol' man standin' right behind him, shaking his bloody head but, slowly, like. And his fuckin' eyes, mate, they'd gone completely fuckin' white. But the worst part was what the gov'nor said."

Edward remained silent, both hands gripping the wheel as best he could despite his increasingly sweaty hands.

"The gov'nor said, 'What old man?'"

"You're pullin' me leg, you fuckin' bastard, you're pullin'..." But by the desolate expression on Quentin's face, Edward knew Quentin was quite serious. He'd gone mad in prison, the poor bloke.

"The ol' man bloody lost it after that. His eyes were always fuckin' white an' empty an' he wouldn't stop wailin' an' moanin' about naughty children. I'd tell him to fuck off and it'd only get worse, he'd get louder, at night he'd be scratchin' the bloody walls cryin' how he had to get out to punish the children. Sometimes at night I'd wake up and he'd be right bloody there in me bed, face to fuckin' face, empty white eyes starin' at me, but then he'd be gone in a flash."

"A real fuckin' wanker."

"And he kept fuckin' hummin' all day the same bloody evil melody, like this." Quentin hummed a dark theme in a minor key.

"Your ol' man's got good taste. That's Rachmaninoff's prelude in C# minor."

Quentin raised an eyebrow in reaction to Edward's unexpected musical knowledge and carried on with his story. "I wanted to get out early on good be'aviour, you know? But the ol' man needed to be put out of his misery."

"The merciful thing to do at that point."

"I took me toothbrush, sharpened the end, and kept it under me pillow. Next time the ol' man would crawl into me bed, I'd take him out."

"Fuckin' ol' man."

"So, it's the middle of the bloody night, and I fuckin' hear him like his voice is comin' from all the fuckin' walls. He was hummin' that bloody tune again. So I open me eyes, and he's right above me in me bed, 'bout an inch away, eyes all white, his bloody mouth wide open, fuckin' rotten teeth in me face, and his throat was like a bloody black hole or somethin' and yet he's still fuckin' yellin' about children an' all that without even movin' his bloody lips."

Edward missed a stop sign despite his eyes being glued to the road. "Fuckin' wanker." His voice trembled.

"So, I went right for the jugular, but me bloody hand went right through his neck, like he was made of some fuckin' cold, damp air, like mist or somethin', but colder. And that made him real angry."

"So, he wasn't real."

"He was a fuckin' ghost, mate."

"Fuck off."

"After I tried to kill him, he grabbed me throat with his disgustin' misty hand, and shouted, 'Bad children must be punished!'"

"You're so full of shit, mate. You can't touch him, but he can grab you?"

"It's a ghost. He's got his own set of rules. But look, I've still got marks along me neck from where he grabbed me."

Quentin pulled down the collar of his shirt, revealing a blue and black handprint, with five scars at the ends of each finger like nails had pierced him around the trachea. The surrounding area was a greenish, rotten colour.

"Looks boss."

Quentin grabbed one of Edward's hands and pressed it against the mark. It burned his hand frozen like it had been soaked in liquid nitrogen. Edward yanked his hand away and said nothing. The silence grew unbearable, and Edward turned on the radio. It played Rachmaninoff's prelude in C# minor. He hurriedly changed the channel, but the prelude played on all of them, growing louder into an invasive crescendo. Quentin plugged his ears with his index fingers as the music grew louder. A sulphurous odour filled the car.

"Your ol' man, he's got empty white eyes, a long beard, an' a crooked nose?" asked Edward.

"Is right, why?" Quentin looked out the windscreen. Only the dark road lay ahead.

Edward was unsure he would manage to respond due to the paralyzing fear taking over him. When he moved his mouth, it felt numb, as though he'd been injected with novocaine. "Just made eye contact with him in the rear-view mirror."

The old man sprang forward from the back seat and seated himself between the driver and passenger's seats. "Naughty children must be punished!"

Quentin and Edward jumped.

The old man vanished, and the car accelerated toward Stanley Wexler, who was riding his bike across Bowsell Street.

"Slow down!" Quentin commanded.

"I'm not doin' anythin'!" said Edward.

Quentin yanked the emergency brake, which merely softened the blow for young Stanley, who was projected off his bike onto the side of the road. The boy's helmet cracked as he struck the asphalt headfirst against the curb. Edward stopped the car, and the two walked over to Stanley's motionless body.

"Should we call an ambulance?" asked Quentin, nudging Stanley with his foot. Stanley moaned, blood dripping out of his mouth.

"Way too bloody bevvied, mate. We'll take him back with us, I'm sure he'll be fine." They picked Stanley up, lay him down along the back seats, and awkwardly shoved his bike in with him. They headed back to Quentin's. Both men stared straight at the road ahead, not saying a word, with only Stanley's erratic breathing breaking the silence. Edward wondered if the smell of metal in the car came from the bike or the child's blood. He rolled down his window. Quentin reached toward the radio but stopped just before turning it on. He didn't want to hear that bloody tune again. He looked at Edward.

"How the fuck does an arse like you know about Rachman-fuck-off's prelude in C# minor?"

*   *   *

Karl Schmidt's tea had gone cold. Dalton McGovern's eyes were lit up and he smiled eagerly, awaiting a reaction from Karl, who felt like a slow pupil. Noticing his anxious enthusiasm, Karl attempted to process the information Dalton had unloaded onto him moments earlier.

"I don't get it," said Karl.

"I don't see what is so hard to understand!" Dalton slammed the table. Karl stayed quiet, his eyebrows raised slightly. Dalton shut his eyes, took a deep breath, and continued. "I'll try to make myself clearer. Using nanotechnology, I have figured out how to map a subject's neural network and recreate the neural network in a simulated environment, essentially uploading the subject's consciousness to a series of servers, or a cloud, if you will." Dalton's eyes lit up once more.

Karl nodded. "Neural... net... yes."

Dalton was growing irritable again. Clearly Karl understood nothing. He got up and put the kettle on.

"How does this make me immortal?" Karl pushed his glasses up the bridge of his nose. "Because it sounds like you'd just be making a copy of my mind, but I myself would be quite dead. None of it would be real."

Dalton's enthusiasm slowly returned, realizing Karl had understood more than he'd expected. "It wouldn't be a simple copy of you. What I am telling you, is it is possible to isolate your mind, your consciousness, and preserve it for all eternity. Death is the expiration of your body. But you know what happens to your consciousness when you die? It lingers in there. In a decaying body. Trapped in an empty void of inexistence until the last light of your brain burns out." The passion in Dalton's eyes faded with that last sentence, as he recalled his own recent experience.

"And how do you expect to get away with what will inevitably be a controversial, unethical project?"

Dalton brought the next serving of hot tea over to the table. "I'm a scientist, not a lawyer. I push boundaries, I don't hide behind regulation that cannot keep up with progress." Dalton poured precisely the same amount of tea into both their cups. He aligned them with one another, handle to handle. Karl had placed sugar cubes in a bowl, which Dalton placed in the centre of the table. He began rearranging the cubes, building a perfect pyramid structure. Karl felt a sudden urge to flick and scatter them. Instead, he took one and placed it into his tea. Dalton immediately fixed the pyramid.

"That's just it though, you're a *computer* scientist. What makes you think you have the expertise to achieve such a thing? You don't know anything about human beings. You can't even interact with them properly without insulting them."

Karl flicked the sugar pyramid. The cubes tumbled down onto the table. Dalton gasped slightly, shut his eyes, and exhaled slowly. He opened his eyes and stared away from the bowl.

"A brain is a computer. Remember when your laptop broke, and you lost all your data? What did I say?" Dalton twitched slightly when he caught a glimpse of the sugar bowl in his peripheral vision.

"That I should have backed my files on a... drive... cloud... thing."

"Very good. In case of a malfunction causing you to lose your data, you should always have a physical and/or cloud backup." Dalton sipped his tea.

"Fine, the brain is a computer, but you still need to play with people's brains. The average computer scientist can't even locate the clitoris." Karl laughed at his own joke, and Dalton shuddered at the thought of the female anatomy. "But please be realistic, Dalton. It's all very fascinating, and I understand you've been in search of a purpose for a while and almost dying was frightening. But you can't play with people's brains based on a personal experience."

"You don't get it!" Dalton crushed one of the fallen sugar cubes against the table. "That's that feeling I had, that my consciousness was lingering around, reaching for any last little spark of life it could grasp. That's what I can recover and preserve." Dalton sat back down. "With the nanotech I've come up with, it will be possible to capture and transfer the mind after death, rendering the subject immortal after living an ordinary life. The mind would then live in a virtual reality for all eternity, which I would create through quantum computer simulation."

"I see. Even if you're dead, your brain still has information you can recover, and you've figured out how to do it."

"Precisely! The brain does not have to be continuously active to survive or retain memory. I can catch the mind at that perfect moment when activity has stopped, but before too much damage has occurred. People live their ordinary lives, die, and come back in the afterlife."

"But what about resources... funding... support... I don't doubt your abilities, but I fear these may be your greatest obstacles." Dalton needed a purpose, and without wanting to discourage him, Karl did want him to lower his expectations.

"Oh, don't patronize me. You think I'm just building myself up in my mind without a plan? I may occasionally have the odd... emotionally difficult moment... but I'm a man of reason." Dalton took the sugar bowl, placed it back in the centre of the table, and began rearranging the cubes again.

"I didn't mean to upset you—"

"There it is again! Upset! Like my reaction comes from emotion and not frustration due to your ignorance! I have a plan."

And as the weeks went by, Dalton's plan proved successful. The first weeks were spent on theories, equations, algorithms, some rubbish about Moore's law and a black-box signal processing model of how neurons respond to nerve impulses. Karl and Darcy saw to the general maintenance of the apartment—and Dalton himself—as he finalized his plan. Next came the begging. Resources. Funding. And sure enough, some scientists from a research initiative based in Switzerland's *École Polytechnique Fédérale de Lausanne* deemed Dalton's plan worthy of starting a sub-project coordinated by the University of Liverpool. The Dean of the School of Electrical Engineering, Electronics and Computer Science told Dalton he could lead the project, but insisted he also teach an introductory linear algebra class.

And then came the animal trials. After a handful of dead rats—Dalton insisted it was all the neurosurgeon's fault—finally, a rat by the name of Clyde survived the insertion of the nanotech into his brain. And when Clyde died a natural death, everyone except Dalton held their breath, waiting to see if he would come back in the simulated reality. Dalton wasn't the least bit doubtful the rat would be back. The neurosurgeon had nothing to do with this part of the process, so surely it would work.

And it did. From a screen, they watched Clyde frolic about in the afterlife, which looked an awful lot like the Albert Dock.

"Don't worry," Dalton told a packed room of observers and reporters gathered at the press conference announcing the breakthrough. "We're still developing the simulated reality. No one is spending all eternity at the Albert Dock."

But Clyde didn't seem to mind. Plenty of places to burrow about.

*   *   *

Stanley Wexler had been missing for the better part of a year. Assuming he was dead, Isidora Prentice tried to focus on her job. However, his mysterious disappearance always seemed to linger in the back of her mind and interfere with work.

Her latest assignment was to investigate a broken window. The cold rain pierced through her jacket as she stood in front of the damaged building.

"Not sure how long it's been like this," said the owner, who stood next to her. "Truth is, I don't really go about fussin' over every little scratch; probably some local lads messing around."

Lads, thought Isidora. *Lads like Stanley.* She tried to focus on the building. Overall, it was poorly maintained. It was surprising he'd even bothered to report the damage to his insurer.

"Look, come inside, I'll show you me'self what broke the window; I haven't touched a thing."

Isidora followed him indoors and observed that not only had he not moved anything around, he hadn't even bothered sweeping up the shattered window glass.

"And it's been like this for how long?"

"A few days, maybe a few weeks, or a month or two or more... Like I said, I don't usually make a fuss... but look." The owner pointed to a shoe on the ground. "That's what did it. Some lad tossed his shoe right through me window."

Isidora picked up the shoe. "It would take a very strong child to throw a little shoe like that hard enough to break a window."

"Sounds like a hard lad!"

"Or rather, the child was not the source of the projection." She ran outside, and the owner followed her, confused yet intrigued.

Isidora's heartbeat quickened, as did her pace of speech. "Say you take a rather stupid child, who runs out of the house without tying his shoes. He gets onto his bike and when he's about... here, he gets hit by a car that had been speeding and had slammed on the brakes a few seconds too late."

The owner's eyes widened.

"He's projected forward off his bike, on a slight angle this way, rotating just over ninety degrees in the air, sending the shoe straight to your window." The owner's eyes followed the imaginary trajectory of the shoe to his window indicated by her pointed finger.

Isidora ran a few steps forward. "The child would have landed just about... here."

She bent down and picked up a jagged piece of plastic sticking from a crack in the nearby gutter. She waved the owner over. He came and bent down next to her. She picked up the piece of plastic and showed it to him.

"Does this look like it could have come from a bicycle helmet to you?"

"Blimey! That's from me mobile!" He pulled out his phone and showed her a chip on the side.

Another day of work meant another day of ridiculous theories for Isidora. After the broken window incident, she accused an arsonist of having killed her nephew in a fire and she suggested an automobile had not hit a pole, as the driver had reported, but rather her nephew. Complaints about Isidora's theories began piling up and her employer was most seriously displeased.

CHAPTER THREE

"Time for brekkie!" Darcy McGovern said, waking up Karl Schmidt, who was asleep on her couch. He had been staying with her since his return to Liverpool.

He sprang up and scooted over to the table like a child on Christmas morning discovering his gifts. Darcy served him a plate of bacon, eggs, sausages, baked beans, and black pudding. He pushed the black pudding to the side with his fork and began eating the rest. Darcy sat down across from him and swallowed a pill with her tea.

"How long will you be on those for?" Karl asked.

"Indefinitely."

"Have you had any episodes recently?"

"Not in ages. I just get the odd headache now."

"Stupid war injury." Karl smiled.

"Stupid war injury." She smiled back, pushed her plate up against Karl's and dragged his black pudding onto her plate with her fork.

Though Darcy did take a bullet to the head in Afghanistan, it merely grazed her just above the ear and left no more than a scrape as an injury. However, since she was rather shaken by the event, and between tours, Karl and Dalton decided to take her on vacation to get her mind off things for a while.

They travelled to Florida, where they stayed far away from any major tourist destination or crowded place in general. They rented a cabin in a remote area, expecting no more than some peace and quiet. However, across the road from them was the most unusual and intriguing property. Large, black gates, about two stories high, surrounded the establishment, and it was impossible to get a glimpse inside. At night, blue sparks from behind the gates would light the sky.

Though they initially ignored their peculiar neighbour, curiosity began to rise among the group. One day, the three walked over to the property to determine once and for all what was going on behind those gates. Darcy gripped the metal slats and attempted to open them, or at the very least, shake them a little. A local man on a hike approached the group.

"You ain't getting through those gates," said the man.

"Why not?" Darcy asked.

"No one goes in, no one goes out. They say a mad man lives in there."

"What kind of mad man?" asked Karl.

"Some say he's a scientist. Others say he's a sorcerer. But there's no way to know for sure."

"A scientist?" said Dalton, his eyes lighting up. "What do you suppose he's up to?"

"Frankly, I don't want to know."

"There's got to be a way in," said Darcy. She pointed to a tall palm tree that stood a couple feet away from the gates. "I bet I could climb that and hop the fence."

The man shook his head. "You can't climb the coconut tree. It's cursed."

"Cursed? How?" asked Darcy.

"One man tried to see over the gates. He fell. Broke his leg. Another man tried to sneak over the gates. He fell. Broke his neck." The man gestured a slicing motion across his own neck. "No one's tried to climb the coconut tree since."

"That doesn't mean it's cursed," said Dalton. "I'm sure if I tried to climb the tree, I would fall as well." Darcy nodded in agreement upon observing Dalton's emaciated figure.

"It's cursed. Haunted by a poltergeist; his sole purpose is to spook intruders away."

"Nonsense," said Karl.

"Believe whatever you want. But I'm telling you, you can't get in there. You can only be invited in. If you try to get in, you'll fail. Go ahead and try... at your own risk."

The man turned away and carried on with his hike.

"Perhaps we should leave," said Karl.

"No way! I want to get in there," said Darcy.

"I must admit, if there is a scientist in there, I would be interested in learning what he's working on," said Dalton.

"It might be a sorcerer," said Darcy.

The gates slowly opened before them. A heavily armed man stood on the other side. Behind him was another, slightly lower set of gates. Nothing was visible on the other side except for a few other palm trees.

"Cash," said the man, holding out his right hand. A hunting rifle was slung over his left shoulder.

Karl looked at Dalton expectantly. Dalton reached into his pocket and handed the man a stack of American bills. He counted it, flipping through the money like he was dealing a deck of cards.

"Five hundred dollars," he said with a frown as he pocketed the cash.

"Yes, I believe so," said Dalton.

"This is an insult to Father Peter. Be gone."

The guard gripped his rifle and fired a few warning rounds on the ground between himself and the group as the gates slowly closed in front of him. They began running across the road. Dalton stumbled and fell over, and Darcy turned to help him get on his feet. They looked back at the gates. With the loud metallic grinding sound of the gates coming to a halt, they were shut out. Never again would the gates open for the group.

"Fuck, Dalton, you blew it for everyone. Always so cheap," said Karl.

"Don't get mad at me. You didn't even want to go inside," said Dalton.

"Let's all just calm down," said Darcy. "I bet I could climb the coconut tree."

"Are you sure that's wise?" asked Karl, while avoiding actually advising against it.

"I'm sure I could manage," she said, walking over to the tree with a hand over her eyes to block out the sun. "I have a feeling there is something special about this place."

Darcy turned around, waiting to see if anyone would try and stop her. The two stood right behind her, saying nothing. She observed how red and freckled they were from the Floridian sun and wondered whether she looked the same.

"Do it," said Dalton.

Darcy gripped the tree with both hands, hopped up, and her feet landed on either side of the trunk. She shimmied up the jagged tree bark without too much trouble until her eyes were nearly level with the top of the gate. While craning her neck to look over, the bark under her left foot broke off, causing both of her feet to slip. She hung on to the trunk only with her arms.

"You're doing great, Darcy, get your feet back on the tree and keep going," said Dalton.

"No way, it's much too dangerous," said Karl. "Darcy, get down from there."

Darcy clasped her legs around the trunk and strengthened her grip.

"I'm nearly there, I can almost see above the gate."

She shimmied up a little higher, and the tree trunk bent slightly forward under her weight. She raised her arms and pulled herself up. The trunk swayed forward even more. She hugged the trunk desperately, fearing now that she would become another victim of the cursed tree. The trunk bent forward until it rested against the gate, stabilizing it. She peered over.

She saw a white, square-shaped mansion with Romanesque columns in front. *Antebellum architecture,* Darcy thought, thinking of all the classic American films set in the Deep South she'd seen. Nothing she'd seen in those films, however, prepared her for the goings-on in the backyard.

She gasped audibly. Hundreds of naked people were milling about, drinking, smoking, and snorting everything imaginable. Guests brought empty champagne glasses over to the fountain and filled them up. Pot plants encircled the estate. The guests began making their way over to something Darcy couldn't quite see.

"What do you see?" Dalton called up.

"Naked people! Plenty of them, partying."

"Brilliant!" said Karl. "We have to find a way inside!"

"Why are they partying?" Dalton asked.

"I'm not sure... they... they seem to be gathering around for something... hang on, I'll try to get a better look."

Darcy shimmied higher until she could see where the guests' attention was directed. A young, surprisingly attractive priest wearing nothing but his collar stood under an altar. On either side of him was a man and a woman, both naked, holding hands. The woman had a large white flower in her wavy, brown hair.

"Dearly beloved, we are gathered here today to join this man and this woman in sinful but holy matrimony," said the priest.

"It's a wedding! A naked wedding!" said Darcy, looking down toward Karl and Dalton. She looked back up to continue viewing the wedding, but the gesture shook the tree trunk a little, causing a coconut to fall into the yard. Captivated by the ceremony, she ignored it.

"I could go on and on about God and love and the afterlife and shit," said the priest, putting an arm around the maid of honour. "But I think the Prince classic, 'Let's Go Crazy,' says it best. Hit it." The song blasted through massive speakers set up around the estate.

The guard who was patrolling the grounds came across the fallen coconut. He looked up.

"Hey, who's there?" he said. He turned his gun toward the coconut tree.

He fired a shot and Darcy jumped straight down from the tree. Karl and Dalton attempted to catch her, but when she landed in their arms, they all fell to the ground with her and ended up with minor to moderately severe injuries. Worst of all was Darcy's concussion, which had her bed-ridden for weeks in a darkened room. From that point on, she would be cursed with migraines.

After the incident, every time she heard so much as a balloon pop, she would remember the Floridian guard trying to shoot her down from the coconut tree. In her dreams he would look for her, tracking her back to Liverpool to punish her for trying to get past the gates. Worse, she could no longer go to church without thinking of the naked priest. It was mortifying when she had to suppress giggles throughout her mother's funeral.

Darcy was eventually diagnosed with post-traumatic stress disorder. However, when she told the story to the psychiatrist, she attributed the gun-related trauma to her close call in Afghanistan. It was far less embarrassing to say she was scarred by war than a coconut tree altercation.

She took Karl's empty plate, piled it on top of her own and brought it over to the counter. They both laughed, recalling the incident.

"I wish I'd seen it for myself," said Karl.

"I don't know. It nearly killed me." Darcy washed the dishes. Karl thought of helping her, but didn't particularly feel like it. He felt good about having had the thought, though.

"I still don't think it was a legally valid wedding."

"Why not? There was a real priest and everything." Darcy dried off the dishes and put them away.

"What sort of priest would perform a naked wedding ceremony quoting Prince?"

Darcy smiled and replied, "All I remember is the guard mentioning someone named Father Peter."

*   *   *

Pope Clement XV hated Father Peter.

Born and raised in the town of Shawinigan, in the French-speaking Canadian province of Québec, the Pope believed in a great deal of things. Strong faith was a necessary quality in a Pope. One thing he believed very strongly was that Québec's French and historically Catholic population was almost entirely doomed to Hell, and worse, assimilation, because of American cultural and economic imperialism.

And that was one of the reasons the Pope hated Father Peter: he was American. Not just American, but *Californian*. The heart of

America's morally corrupt cultural industry.

But the Pope had other reasons to hate Father Peter. Father Peter was a smug bastard that deserved to be excommunicated ages ago. Father Peter made the Pope wish he could bring back burning heretics at the stake, just for him. But since Father Peter was the Church's best exorcist, the Pope tried his very best to be friends with Father Peter.

He made the mistake of introducing Father Peter to his niece, Ève-Marie.

Now, Ève-Marie and Father Peter were raising a bastard child together and maintained a long-distance, polyamorous relationship between Shawinigan and wherever Father Peter was off to next, performing exorcisms for the Church. The Pope had to endure entire family dinners with the unbearable Father Peter. Ève-Marie even had the audacity to say that Father Peter's bastard resembled His Holiness! *Il serait trop mignon habillé comme le Pape, avec le beau p'tit chapeau et la belle grande robe*, she would say, bouncing the drooling creature on her lap.

How the Pope hated Father Peter. And there he sat, looking smug as ever, in the Vatican's reading room, carelessly flipping through pages of ancient scripture, laughing at the illuminated manuscripts to which generations of monks had dedicated their lives. The Pope walked under the golden archways of the great room, surrounded by some of the finest works of art in Europe. A stream of light burst through one of the arched windows and shone upon Father Peter, who was seated in the back of the empty room at one of its many long, wooden tables. The Pope sat down across him, waiting to see if Father Peter would so much as look up from the manuscript. Father Peter laughed some more.

"Look, Your Holiness. Clearly this monk had never seen a naked chick." He turned the book towards the Pope, inadvertently tearing out a page. "My bad." He crumpled the page in a ball and tossed it aimlessly over his shoulder.

The Pope grabbed the book and slammed it shut. The violent echo stunned Father Peter briefly, but shortly after, he laughed some more. The Pope stared into Father Peter's comical blue eyes until he felt he had his full attention. It was taking a while. He glared. Father Peter smiled. *Smug bastard.* The Pope reached forward, grabbed Father Peter by the throat and stood up slowly, pulling up Father Peter with him. The Shawinigan handshake.

Once Father Peter was sufficiently purple, he let him go. The Pope sat back down as Father Peter massaged his neck. The two burst into laughter.

"Your Holiness, I suppose you summoned me here for a specific reason, and not just because you enjoy the pleasure of my company so much." Father Peter fixed his collar and ran his hand through his golden curls. The Pope found him terribly effeminate.

"I was going over a report that you did," said the Pope, his thick Québécois accent emphasizing his broken English. "Now I remember how you are saying that a proper exorcism is not really so easy to do, because you are not on the same 'spiritual dimension' as the demon?"

"Correct, Your Holiness. It's not impossible or anything, but it's a bit like fighting blind."

The Pope grunted. "So, you are seeing better the demon if you are also a celestial being?"

"Yeah, exactly. That's why in my report, I suggest that the ideal exorcist would be someone capable of detaching his soul from his body." As much as he loved his body, Father Peter knew this would make his job much simpler.

The Pope pushed his phone over to Father Peter. "I got some good news. I saw it in Tweeter," he said, pointing to the screen.

"Twitter," corrected Father Peter.

"Shut up and listen, you smug bastard. There is this... crazy guy... in Liverpool saying to everyone he can upload a person's 'consciousness' in an 'afterlife' he is making up in his computer games." The Pope and Father Peter laughed together. They both knew perfectly well that the conscious mind was merely the manifestation of the soul. "At first, I say, whatever, this crazy guy. But then I see that he is doing it to a rat and it work!"

"How does he do it, exactly?" asked Father Peter. "I know in the past, mind uploading seemed doomed to fail, that the human mind couldn't survive such a transfer of information. You and I know that's because separating a person's soul from their body kills them.

So, how did he do it without killing the rat?"

"You know when a person die, their soul sort of floats a little before moving on? He trap it then with some computer shit and put it in the computer," the Pope explained.

Father Peter nodded approvingly. "He sounds like a smart dude. Of course, trapping souls in a computer program sounds like something that would piss off the Heavens. Should we do something?"

The Pope shrugged. "At first, I think, we cannot let this crazy guy do this shit. But then I remember your report, and I am thinking, we can maybe use this technology instead. I want you to try it, see if once your soul is detached, it is easier to do an exorcism."

Father Peter began biting his fingernails. He was deeply ashamed of this particular habit, but luckily his manicurist was most forgiving. "I would need to break out of the computer system to be free to go around performing exorcisms. And I would have to be dead for him to trap my soul in the system."

The Pope smiled at the thought of Father Peter being dead. "You know how the Heavens can be. I think anyone who puts that thing in his head will die soon after. And then I bet the Heavens will fight the computer system to get the souls."

"But then I would just go to Heaven."

The Pope laughed at the idea of Father Peter going to Heaven. "I think it will not be so simple. You know better than anybody how determined souls can be to stay put when they have some weird death. This is the weirdest death I can think of, so I think it will give you some room for manoeuvring."

Father Peter nodded, remembering the last soul he'd exorcised. Hiding in the child, then the dog, then the oven... that last host was particularly dangerous.

"But! You must keep it a secret since it is all so weird," the Pope continued. "Officially, you will go to Liverpool for a traditional exorcism. There is some stupid murderer guy who got this old man spirit attached to his neck while he was in prison and he took it home with him. The doctor is saying he is not crazy, and the local bishop is saying it is a real possession case. So, officially, this is why you go to Liverpool. Then, you go see the crazy guy and sign up for his experiment."

Father Peter and the Pope shook on the plan with the secret Holy Handshake, a gesture more binding than any legal contract. After their meeting, they headed out for some gelato and a walk around the Vatican gardens. A visiting cardinal spotted Father Peter and dropped to his knees before him. "*Tu eres el!* You are the one!" he said, holding out his arms to Father Peter. The priest smiled and gave him a wink.

The Pope snapped his fingers and members of the Swiss Guard dragged the cardinal away.

"You cannot suppress the truth forever, Clement!" cried the cardinal, his voice fading away.

Father Peter ate his gelato and carried on. It wasn't uncommon for such things to occur in his presence. He didn't stop to question it; he figured his stellar reputation as an exorcist had earned him some kind of cult following.

The Pope looked at Father Peter eating his gelato and observed that the smug bastard didn't even question such outbursts of veneration. Somewhere, Father Peter was beginning to grow on him. The Pope loved to hate Father Peter.

CHAPTER FOUR

"**B**ugger off, the lot of you!" Darcy McGovern didn't appreciate the small group of protesters bothering her brother and his team outside the doors of the university's AI laboratory. They were making it difficult for her to bring Dalton his lunch.

"You should be ashamed!" said a man holding up a sign that read *No Human Trials*.

Darcy rolled her eyes. First, it had been the animal rights people insisting not to test the afterlife on the rats. Now, it was the religious fanatics losing their minds over human trials. Karl had been right about it being a headache, ethically speaking. Though it was also proving to be a literal headache. Darcy tried to ignore the throbbing at her temples which announced the beginning of a migraine.

"I'm a little bit psychic and I have a feeling my brother forgot to make his lunch today, so I'd like to bring him one, if you don't mind," Darcy told one protester. *I served our country defending your bloody rights and this is what you do with them?* Darcy thought hard, hoping the man would hear her on some level.

"Jesus saves!" exclaimed a woman who gave Darcy a pamphlet explaining the miracle of Christ. Darcy tossed it on the ground but felt guilty about littering and picked it back up.

"I'm Catholic. And look what the Pope tweeted!" Darcy pulled out her phone and showed it to the woman and the other protesters. Indeed, the Pope had written: "I hear some stupid American televangelists saying to stop some crazy guy in Liverpool. But God said, no don't bother with that." Darcy wondered why the Pope wrote his own tweets.

"Papist!" the woman shouted. Darcy rolled her eyes again and elbowed her way past them. She walked into the lab.

Dalton and his team were watching Clyde burrow about in his virtual afterlife. The latest development was that Clyde could now generate certain things he wanted in the simulated reality. The Albert Dock was full of grains, seeds and fruit for Clyde to nibble on. He was also capable of changing certain things about himself he didn't like. For reasons only Clyde knew, he had chosen not to have a tail anymore.

"Dr. McGovern!" a dark-haired, bug-eyed neurosurgeon, Dr. Fanny Whalen, called out to Dalton as she entered the lab, waving around a dead rodent high in the air. "Brooke died!"

"Excellent," replied Dalton. "It shouldn't be long before she joins Clyde." All eyes were now glued to the screen, waiting for a second little grey rat to appear. Sure enough, Brooke showed up in the simulated reality and began eating from Clyde's abundance of seeds. The team applauded.

"This is starting to make me hungry," said Dalton, going through his bag.

"I've got you covered," said Darcy, bringing him the lunch she'd made him.

"Creepy twins anticipating each other's needs," observed Dr. Fanny Whalen.

Darcy jerked her head in Dr. Whalen's direction, but her eyes seemed to lose focus. "You're going to die a painful death rather soon, I'm afraid," Darcy uttered to her in a low, monotone voice.

Dr. Whalen shuddered and dropped the dead rat on the floor. "Like I said, twins are creepy," she muttered under her breath.

Karl hurried to join Dalton and Darcy, holding his laptop. In his rush, he nearly tripped over a wire on the floor. The only thing that kept him from falling was the fear of breaking the computer, which still wasn't backed onto any sort of cloud, despite Dalton's advice. He pulled up a chair between the two and sat down, placing the computer on his lap.

"Look, we've got it!" said Karl. "Authorization for human trials. Now all we need is the consent of a few competent and capable adults."

Dalton nodded. "Thank you for dealing with all the legalities, Karl. I understand it hasn't been particularly easy."

Karl had hardly slept in the past eight months trying to find a way around the unethical nature of the experiment. "Oh, it was nothing, really."

Clyde approached Brooke, hoping she might be interested in mating. She grew three times his size, hissed, and left with his food. He generated some more.

"Poor ol' sod. Looks like you can't have everything you want, even in Heaven," said Darcy.

Dr. Fanny Whalen had been eavesdropping. "Competent and consenting adults. Right. I can't imagine what kind of competent adult would consent to such an experiment."

"Souls doomed to a fate worse than death," Darcy said in the same flat voice as before. Dalton, Karl and Dr. Whalen looked at her with widened eyes. Even Darcy seemed taken aback by her words. They all quietly turned back towards the large screen. Brooke was now swimming in the River Mersey.

*   *   *

"Bottle or tap?"

Isidora Prentice stood behind the bar, waiting for the greasy man sitting on a stool on the other side to decide what to order. The Toxteth pub was dimly lit and needed renovations, but Isidora didn't care enough to bring it up with the owner. Most people came to the pub to place bets on football games. The average clientele was middle-aged men who enjoyed looking at Isidora almost as much as they enjoyed watching football, which they enjoyed almost as much as drinking.

"Bottle. No, tap. No... How much are they?"

"Five pounds for a bottle. Four-fifty for a pint."

The man pulled out a pile of change from his pocket and began counting. He'd nearly finished, lost count, and restarted. Isidora had already had the time to count twice that he had four pounds, seventy pence in total, but figured it would be rude to interrupt him. Isidora was working on her patience with customers. The questionable people she served at the pub reminded her of the questionable people she used to investigate in her former job.

The greasy man counted the change once more to be sure he'd gotten it right, this time on his fingers. He nodded once he was confident he'd counted it properly.

"Bottle, please."

Isidora didn't move. "You sure about that?"

The man looked at the change and hesitated.

"I'll get you a pint," said Isidora.

Isidora took a pint glass out of the fridge and filled it with the darkest beer available. She placed it on a coaster and pushed it over to the greasy man.

"I haven't seen you here before. Are you new?" the man asked Isidora.

"Yes and no." She hated the small talk she had to make with customers.

"What's that mean?"

"I worked here until I was twenty-one. I didn't expect I would be back six years later."

A Welsh construction worker seated two seats away from the greasy man laughed. "They always come back," he said.

"So I was told, when I left."

"What brought you back, luv?" asked the greasy man. He drank a quarter of his pint in one swig and slammed it loudly against the table.

"Got sacked." Isidora attempted to make eye contact with him, but his focus was on her chest.

"Why's that? What divvy, that boss of yours," said the man, looking her up and down.

"My nephew went missing and I couldn't concentrate on my work anymore."

"Your nephew's missing? Is he a Liverpool lad?" asked the Welsh construction worker.

Isidora nodded and took the empty pint in front of him away.

"Another?" she asked. He nodded. She got a new glass out of the fridge, filled it and handed it to him.

"This might not mean anything," said the Welsh man, "but, over at me neighbours', I sometimes hear some man shouting things about naughty children at night. Like I said, it doesn't really mean anythin', but—"

"Where?" asked Isidora.

He wrote the address down on a napkin and handed it to her. He had added his number and a heart. She put it in her pocket. Though the most likely scenario was that it was an attempt to seduce her, or perhaps murder her in his home, Isidora had already come up with a new theory that her nephew had been kidnapped by a mad man who wanted to punish naughty children. Stanley had never been particularly well behaved.

After her afternoon shift ended, Isidora decided to head directly to the address written on the napkin. It was pouring rain but she didn't bother to flag down a cab, deciding to walk instead, even though she had neither a raincoat nor brolly. She turned down a narrow alley that smelled of sulphur The closer she got to her destination, the stronger grew the smell. She arrived at the flat and knocked aggressively.

The door swung open and she looked up at the man standing on the other side of the threshold. His dark, greying hair matched his stubble beard, and the lines that framed the corners of his dark eyes and thin lips conveyed the benumbed maturity born of hardship. The sulphurous odour emitting from the apartment was so strong Isidora chose to breathe only from her mouth, but instantly regretted it after taking in the air that tasted of rotten eggs. She tried not to gag.

"Oi, Quentin! Who's that?" a voice inside the apartment shouted.

Quentin looked Isidora up and down. "Wow, very nice! I wasn't expectin' a woman; I thought only men could be priests," he said. He turned around. "Eddie, come have a look at this."

A priest? Does he really think I'm a priest? How could he possibly mistake me for a priest? thought Isidora, looking down at her outfit, wondering if anything about her short, tight, black, soaking wet dress or her bright-red heels gave him the impression she had taken an oath of chastity. *Fuck it, just go with it.*

"They've changed the rules around a bit," said Isidora, stepping into the flat. It was small, damp, and in addition to the smell of sulphur, she detected a strong odour of rum and cigarettes. "Got a ciggy?" she asked.

Edward Reid raced over and handed her his entire pack. "All yours, gorgeous." She began to smoke, waiting for one of them to say something.

"So the ol' man... not sure where he is, but he'll pop up soon, he always does," said Quentin.

Isidora observed him closely. *What a harsh look. Must have broken his nose several times. Not bad looking, though, overall.* She looked at his tattoos, covering his fingers up to his neck. *Prison tattoos. Strangeways? No, probably Liverpool. Hang on, his neck... What the bloody hell is that?*

"Oh, there he is over on the couch, the ol' man!" said Edward. "Wait, he's not usually dressed so..."

"What a clean old man!" said Isidora. Holding a book, the old man was sitting with a polite little smile on his face. His beard was gone, and his eyes were a warm green. He wore reading glasses on his crooked nose. He waved to her and went back to reading his book.

"Stan!" Quentin called. "The priest...ess... is here! Come see, she's really somethin'!"

Stanley Wexler limped upstairs from the basement, a cigarette at his lips and a can of beer in his hand. His entire body was covered in linear red scars, giving him the appearance of a human road map.

"Oh, bullocks," Stanley said. "That's no priestess, that's me bitch aunt Isidora."

Before she could react, Edward grabbed her by the hair, pulled her head back against his shoulder and pressed a switchblade against her cheek. She could smell the beer on his breath. He cut her slightly along the cheekbone.

"Not a sound or I'll cut yer tongue out," he said.

She elbowed him. He let go of her hair and quickly locked her arms behind her back. She struggled against him helplessly.

Stanley laughed. "Do it! Cut her!" he said.

"Look, we can explain," Quentin said to Isidora. "It's not what it looks like. It's all the ol' man's fault."

Stanley was growing frustrated. "She's a real bitch and deserves to lose her tongue for all the shit she says. Do it, Eddie, or I'll do it me'self!"

The old man put his book down and made his way over to Stanley, who turned away.

"That's no way to talk to a lady," said the old man. Stanley tried hard to hold back tears, sniffling and cowering. The old man bent down to Stanley's eye level and moved from side to side, trying to make eye contact, but Stanley kept avoiding the old man's eyes. "I think that kind of language deserves punishment."

"Christ, not again," said Quentin.

"Sir," Isidora said to the old man. "These men have kidnapped my nephew. Please, help us!"

The old man turned around and made his way over to Isidora. *There's something strange about the way he walks,* she thought, and looked at his feet. He was hovering slightly, gliding over the floor. She looked back up and his face was now only half an inch away from hers. His green eyes slowly began to fade away.

"If you're his aunt, why didn't you *discipline* him?" he said, his voice booming and resonating around the room. His eyes had emptied of all colour.

Isidora swallowed but managed to maintain a steady voice. "He's not my child. He's not my problem. I'm only here now as a favour to my sister."

Edward's grip softened. He slowly moved his arms and held her gently over the shoulders and across the chest, protectively. The old man's beard began to grow back, and his little reading glasses disappeared. He grimaced, showing her his rotten, yellow teeth.

"With your hair and beard like that, you look a bit like Karl Marx. Has anyone ever told you that?" said Isidora.

Quentin laughed. Edward and Stanley looked at each other in horror, imagining how the old man might react to her attitude. In a split second, his mouth opened wide enough to swallow her entire head. His breath's cold, misty texture against her face burned her eyes and skin like bleach and its sulphurous smell made her stomach churn. He emitted a piercing cry, and suddenly vanished. Stanley limped over to Isidora and wrapped his arms around her waist, in tears. She didn't hug him back, although she patted him twice on the head.

Someone knocked on the door. Edward gestured for Isidora to remain quiet, opened the door and stood face to face with Father Peter. The priest wore blue jeans and a leather jacket. He smiled, flashing his perfect, straight, white teeth. It made Edward jealous. The priest's curly hair had been flattened by the rain, and his bright blue eyes playfully scanned the flat. He held in one hand what looked like a toolbox with a large white cross painted on it. In the other, he held a pack of beer.

"Someone called for an exorcism?"

*   *   *

"No, not this one," said Darcy, as yet another candidate for human trials walked into Dalton's office for an interview.

Dalton, Karl, who was acting as legal counsel, and Dr. Fanny Whalen, the neurosurgeon, were meeting with each candidate one at a time. After the first dozen meetings, they brought in Darcy for security. The team had learned that it is not always Great Britain's most mentally stable citizens who sign up for such experiments.

"Seriously, Darcy, you're going to have to stop doing that every time a candidate walks through the door. It messes with our judgment," griped Dalton.

"I felt the energies of the ones you'd end up choosing and this isn't the right energy!"

Dr. Whalen looked at Dalton, and then at Karl, widening her eyes, hoping to find they agreed that Darcy was just as mad as she thought. They ignored her. A plump woman with an entirely pink face sat in front of the three, waiting for her interview to begin.

"Sorry about that, Ms. Brighton. It's been a long day. I'm Karl, and these are my colleagues, Dr. McGovern and Dr. Whalen."

"Oh, aren't you a handsome devil, you!" said Ms. Brighton, leaning forward to pinch Karl's cheek. "After me heart with that cheeky little grin and sweet little accent!" She tapped his cheek twice and giggled.

"That will be all. Thank you for your time," said Dalton through his teeth.

Ms. Brighton stayed seated. She'd hardly had time to process Dalton's immediate rejection when Darcy showed her out of the room.

"Go along now, your energy's all wrong," Darcy said, escorting Ms. Brighton to the door. "Have a lovely day!" she added, as Ms. Brighton shuffled off.

Darcy brought in the next candidate. "This one too, he's all wrong, his aura is much too string-like. The ones you will pick are more circular."

A dapper older man shook hands with all three and sat down. He apologized for having his hat on indoors, removed it, and lightly dusted off the elbow patches of his navy-blue sweater.

"You must be Mr. Owens," said Dr. Whalen, picturing how she'd slice up his brain should he be selected for human trial.

"Oh, why, you can call me Don!" he said. "Not sure if it's me real name, but I like the sound of it."

After a brief pause, Karl decided it was his duty to ask the next question, as the only person in the room with social skills. "So... Don... what interests you about the work we're doing here?"

"I read the ideal candidate was someone older, or near death, so that you yourselves could oversee the initial human trials when the time should come."

Dalton nodded with some excitement. *Finally, a promising candidate.*

"I was diagnosed with Alzheimer's disease last year, and I've made me peace with death. It would mean the world to me to be able to meet me grandchildren one day, even in a virtual world."

"No, no, definitely not," said Karl. "He doesn't have the capacity to consent. We'll get sued. Darcy, please, if you will," he said, gesturing towards the door.

He felt terribly guilty immediately after the words had slipped out; Mr. Owens' eyes welled up with tears. *Legal paranoia trumps good social skills, apparently,* Karl thought.

"Your grandchildren will certainly enjoy photos and videos and plenty of other lovely memorabilia," Karl added. "You seem very kind, Mr. Owens, I'd love to get to know you better!"

Mr. Owens walked away with his head down. Darcy put an arm around him and consoled him as she escorted him out of the building.

"And you say I'm bad with people," said Dalton. Karl held his head between his hands.

"I just want to get in there, already. Cut cut," said Dr. Whalen, making a sawing gesture with her hands.

Dalton leaned slightly away from her, toward Karl. "Perhaps we should call it a day."

CHAPTER FIVE

"Open wide."

Father Peter flashed a light down Quentin's throat. "Mhm. Mhmmmm."

He pulled down Quentin's lower eyelids and stared at his eyes with a magnifying glass.

"I see," said Father Peter. He tapped each of Quentin's knees with the magnifying glass, causing his leg to straighten up. "Reflexes look good," he said. Quentin couldn't help but question the priest's methods.

Edward, Stanley, and Isidora stood back, watching the examination, keeping an eye out for the old man. Isidora, smoking her seventh cigarette since entering the apartment, passed it to Edward, who then passed it to Stanley.

"It helps with me nerves," Stanley explained before Isidora could question him on the habit.

"I wasn't going to say anything."

Father Peter pulled out a syringe and plunged it into Quentin's neck. Quentin shut his eyes and pursed his lips as Father Peter drained a dark fluid out of the handprint the old man had left. The mark on Quentin's neck faded away.

"Ahh, much better," said Father Peter.

The priest reached into his bag and pulled out what looked like a cocktail shaker. He poured the liquid from the syringe into the shaker and shook it over one shoulder, flipped it behind his back with one hand and caught it with the other. He took a glass out of his toolbox and poured the liquid content of the shaker, which had turned pink, into it, filtering the ice out with two strainers.

"Drink this," said Father Peter. "The demon's evil fluid has been mixed in with one ounce of holy water, one ounce of lemon juice, one ounce of simple syrup, and two ounces of gin. It's a bit like a vaccine; it will strengthen your immune system against future hauntings."

Quentin looked at Edward, who shrugged and nodded. Stanley gave him two thumbs up. He chugged the drink in a few seconds and high fived Father Peter upon emptying the glass.

"That might be a new record," said Father Peter.

"So that's it, then? No more old man?" asked Quentin.

"Oh, no, we're just getting started. That probably just made him violently angry. But the good news is, you're not exactly possessed. He just sort of latched himself onto you, so this should be relatively painless." Father Peter stood up and looked around the flat. "The problem is, we have to find him. What normally brings him out?"

Stanley raced over to Father Peter and kicked him in the shin. "That should do it," said Stanley.

"Atta boy!" said Edward.

Rachmaninoff's prelude in C# minor began to resonate from the walls of the flat. The lights flickered, until they all went out.

"That's way too spooky," said Father Peter. "We can't let him set the scene. Can someone put some music on?"

Quentin took out his phone, which was connected to the sound system, and hit shuffle. Stevie Wonder's "Superstition" came on.

"Funny coincidence," Quentin said.

"My friend," said Father Peter, taking a copy of the Bible out of his toolbox. "There are no such things as coincidences. That—" the priest pulled out a thurible and waved it around, and burning incense filled the room with smoke, "—was fate."

Father Peter tossed his jacket on the ground and rolled up his black sleeves.

"Naughty children must be punished!"

The old man appeared behind Stanley, snatched the cigarette out of the boy's mouth and pressed the burning end to the flesh of the boy's inner forearm.

"Bad child! Nasty child!" said the old man, as Stanley bit his lip and blinked back tears.

Isidora slapped the cigarette away from Stanley's arm like she was swatting a bee. It fell to the ground, still burning.

The old man shook his fist in her face. "Know your place, woman," he growled.

"A demon and a sexist," she observed. "Lovely."

The old man leaned close to Isidora and licked her behind the ear with a tongue as cold as an icicle. She shuddered from the misty, freezing sensation of his tongue touching her skin and gagged as she caught a whiff of his foul breath.

Father Peter cleared his throat. "If I could have just a minute of your time, I'd like to tell you about our Lord and Saviour, Jesus Christ."

The old man screeched. He dove through the air towards Father Peter, his dark mouth wide open. Father Peter held up a cross.

"You think a stick can stop me, useless servant of God?" hissed the old man.

"Well, I've sharpened the bottom of it." He stabbed the old man in the back of the throat with the cross.

"Did you learn to do that in prison?" asked Quentin.

"Yes," said Father Peter.

The old man cowered briefly, then sank his rotten teeth into the priest's arm. Father Peter smacked him on the head with the Bible and freed himself.

"All right, you might want to take a few steps back, I'm going to open the gates of Hell soon," said Father Peter.

Isidora pulled Stanley back. Edward stayed put, so she yanked him back, too.

"Oh, hold up!" Father Peter took out some sheets of paper from his toolbox and handed them out to everyone. "We can all say the prayer together."

The four moaned.

"Oh, come on, guys, is church that boring?" asked Father Peter.

They nodded.

"Well, it isn't when I'm celebrating Mass," he said as he stabbed the old man in each of his eyes a couple times.

"All together now!" said Father Peter, starting the exorcism prayer. "In the name of the Father, and the Son, and the Holy Spirit, Amen."

"Boring," said Stanley.

The old man giggled evilly. "You see, Father? He's a naughty child, very disrespectful. He should be punished."

Father Peter stabbed the old man in the ear with the cross. "We drive you from us, whoever you may be, unclean old man."

"He seemed clean at first," said Isidora, embarrassed by her initial assessment.

"It's time for you to fuck off back to Hell now." Father Peter reached into his toolbox and pulled out a paintball rifle loaded with capsules full of holy water.

"God the Father commands you!"

Holding the gun with one hand, Father Peter shot the old man in the stomach. The old man hissed an old Aramaic curse word and clutched his abdomen.

"God the son commands you!"

Father Peter shot him in the hip, and the old man dropped to his knees.

"God the Holy Ghost commands you!"

Father Peter shot him in the chest, and the old man collapsed to the ground like a fall-down drunk. The priest walked over to the wheezing old man, who held up his hand defensively.

"Is this the part where you expect me to beg for mercy?" he growled, an acidic green substance oozing out of his wounds. The smell of sulphur in the apartment grew even stronger.

Father Peter pointed the gun between the old man's eyes. "Begone, old man!"

Father Peter shot him down. Holy Water drenched the demon and his facial muscles began to contort. A tremor followed that shook the floor beneath their feet and the sound of thunder boomed throughout the apartment. The floorboards directly under the old man began to smoulder and break apart. A dark, seemingly bottomless pit below the old man opened up. He levitated, grasped at the air and kicked around as if he were trying to keep from falling into the abyss. The sweltering heat of a thousand furnaces filled the room. A musky, sweet aroma combined with a coppery, metallic smell overwhelmed the sulphurous odour. Cries of terror and agony echoed from the void.

"Smells like burning bodies," Quentin remarked.

"How do you know what a burning body smells like?" asked Isidora. He looked at her, winked, and did not provide an answer.

From the shadowy void sprang black tentacles oozing with green acid. They slowly wrapped around the old man's body, like a snake with its prey, and dragged him down to Hell. The hole shut tight and the lights came on.

"That was brilliant!" said Stanley. "The old man got eaten by an alien. And the priest was like a cowboy in an American Western."

Who could ever want to punish this kid? thought Father Peter, as Stanley limped over to the fridge and cracked open another can of beer for himself.

*   *   *

Darcy invited Dalton over for dinner nearly every day, but he typically refused, claiming he had to focus on his work. However, after another day went by without finding the right candidates for his experiment, and with mounting pressure from stakeholders and lobbyists demanding that the government pass a bill to render his experiment illegal, he was ready to take a moment to get his mind off the afterlife.

He sat at the kitchen table with his twin sister and his ex-boyfriend. Karl looked disgusted by the steak and kidney pie at the table. *Typical Karl, nothing is ever good enough for him,* Dalton thought. He reached for a bottle of cider and Darcy snatched it out of his hand.

"The doctor said you aren't supposed to drink with your medication," she said.

Dalton hadn't taken any of the medication he'd been prescribed and didn't intend to take anything that could alter his perfect mind. But, he figured it was best his sister didn't know, or she would never leave him alone. Unlike her, Dalton didn't intend on sitting around all day doing nothing but collecting paycheques from the government on the basis of a so-called disability. The world needed him.

"Of course. I'd forgotten." Dalton bitterly contented himself with a glass of water.

"Since when do you forget anything?" Karl asked.

"It must be your daily presence, slowly killing my hippocampus cells."

Karl's phone rang. He excused himself and left the kitchen.

"You don't have to talk to him like that. He came back to help you," said Darcy.

"I never asked him to come back."

"Yes, you did, love," said Darcy, thinking of his suicide attempt. "You just have a funny way of asking people for things."

Dalton got up from his chair and left the room. Darcy was too invasive; he couldn't stand being alone with her. She would always get far too personal, wanting to talk about his problems, when she should have been marvelling at his successes of late. He didn't have problems; he had solutions. He approached Karl, who was talking on the phone, standing in Darcy's room with his back turned to the doorway.

"Stop calling me Hitler and stop calling me altogether. Goodbye."

Karl hung up on the caller and turned. Dalton stood in the doorway. Startled, he dropped his phone on the floor. It bounced a couple of times and landed at Dalton's feet. Dalton started to bend down to pick it up for him, but Karl lurched forward, grabbed it and shoved it in his pocket.

"Who was that?" asked Dalton.

"Just some children. Some kind of practical joke, I imagine."

Dalton frowned. "Was it necessary to leave the dinner table to take that call? You can't leave me alone with her; it's terribly awkward."

"And it makes it less awkward to have me at the table with you?" Karl smiled.

"Yes, because the two of you can talk to each other instead of bothering me with questions about my problems."

Karl stepped out of the room and stood in the doorway with Dalton.

"We just want to help, you know."

Dalton crossed his arms. "I get what's going on with the two of you. You both live pathetic, meaningless lives, and caring for me gives you a sense of purpose. You want to be part of my greatness; you latch onto me and give yourselves credit for my accomplishments. Like I wouldn't have managed without you two. Though, it's more insidious than that. It's also a way of putting me down and feeling superior to me. Poor fragile Dalton can't take care of himself; good thing he's surrounded by such loving people who help him heal and improve himself! I'm not your bloody pet. Quit expecting me to wag my tail and be eternally grateful for your generosity and care. Both of you, just leave me alone."

Dalton stormed out of Darcy's flat and slammed the door behind him. He flagged down a cab, took a seat in the back and checked his emails on his phone. He'd received multiple adoring messages from his students at the university, asking to meet with him during his office hours to learn more about his work. He smiled at his phone.

Meanwhile, Darcy and Karl cleared the table. Using his fork, Karl had broken his slice of pie into several pieces, hoping it looked like he'd eaten something. Darcy pretended she fell for his ruse, took the plate, and put it on the ground. Darcy's bulldog, Alfred, buried his wrinkled face into the dish. She began washing the remainder of the dishes.

"He's not well at all," said Karl, drying off the clean dishes.

"Oh, don't worry, he eats all sorts of things," said Darcy, looking at her fat dog.

"No, I meant Dalton. Dalton is unwell."

"I know, I can still feel the emptiness inside of him. It's the same emptiness I'd felt from me ma, before... well, you know." Darcy handed another plate over to Karl for drying.

"I don't think he'll ever get to that point. He's far too proud to accept such a chaotic existence. He'd sooner kill himself."

"Is right."

Karl's phone rang again. He answered it and walked away,

leaving Darcy alone with the rest of the dishes.

*   *   *

The right thing to do would have been to take Stanley back home. But the natural thing to do after witnessing an exorcism was to have a drink. Father Peter was always prepared to put his mixology skills to use. An Old Fashioned for Quentin and Edward, a Whisky Sour for Isidora, a Tom Collins for Stanley and a Martini Gibson for himself. They shared drinks around an uneven wooden table designed for two people.

"I wasn't possessed?" asked Quentin.

"No, but I'm sure that's what he hoped to do. Demons prey on the vulnerable, the mentally ill, children... judging by the look of you, he chose a terrible host."

Edward patted Quentin on the back forcefully, yet amicably. "He was always the hardest lad around back in school and he's even harder today. Harder than him, you'd be made of bloody kryptonite."

Isidora laughed and finished her drink in a few seconds. Edward frowned.

"You think I'm jokin'?" he asked.

"No, I believe he's as hard as you say," said Isidora. She looked at Quentin and smiled, then turned to Edward. "You, on the other hand... Despite appearances, I believe you're the sort of man who collects comic books."

Edward frowned and spat.

"Perhaps you even dress up as your favourite character at conventions for like-minded individuals," she hypothesized.

Quentin laughed. "A clever one, she is," he said and looked at Isidora. She brought her empty glass to her lips, seeking out any last traces of her cocktail. Unsuccessful, she put the glass back down.

"When I grow up, I want to be an exorcist, just like Father Peter!" said Stanley. He formed the shape of a gun with his fingers and pretended to shoot Isidora, imitating the sound of a gun. She smacked his hands down.

"There's a secret training centre for young boys in the Vatican, if you're really interested. The Exorcist Academy is as prestigious as it is secret," said Father Peter.

Stanley turned to Quentin, placed his hands together as though he were praying and said "please" repeatedly.

"No, no, definitely not," said Quentin. "Sounds like a bloody trap. We didn't get rid of one pedophile just to send him to an academy full of 'em."

"We aren't pedophiles!" said Father Peter. "Since Pope Clement XV made it an unofficial rule to turn a blind eye to consenting adult relations, the priesthood has become a far less creepy career path."

"Oh, yes, I remember that tweet," said Isidora. She scrolled through her phone and found it. "Sex and stuff, no kids or animals or family or weird shit in animal costumes. Other than that, whatever, leave me alone, I'm sick of hearing about your sex lives," she read aloud.

"Apparently his niece Ève-Marie is off limits, though," mumbled Father Peter.

"So? Can I go to the Academy?" Stanley asked Quentin, who shrugged and looked at Father Peter.

"You know, he's not your father," said Isidora.

Stanley threw his drink on the floor and the glass shattered. "How do you know? Mum's never told me who me dad is. Could be him."

Isidora observed Quentin's dark eyes, black, greying hair, strong jawline and slim, athletic build, in contrast with Stanley's frizzy blond hair, wide blue eyes and chubby red cheeks. *Unlikely*, she thought.

Edward raised his eyebrows. "Is your mum as pretty a bird as your auntie here?" he asked Stanley.

"Disgustin'!" said Stanley. "Both Mum and Auntie Izzy are fat and ugly and stupid." He turned to Quentin. "Can I please, please, please be an exorcist?"

"I don't see why not," said Quentin. "What do you think, Father?"

"Perhaps we could work something out," said Father Peter. "I'll be right back. I have to call the Pope. I'll ask him directly." He went downstairs.

"Since when is that your decision to make?" Isidora asked Quentin.

"Well it's not yours either, but Stan likes me better than you."

Stanley nodded and lit another cigarette for himself. Isidora went downstairs to interrupt Father Peter's conversation.

"Yes, Your Holiness, I'll go see him tomorrow. I've already scheduled a meeting. The team's lawyer had an awful lot of questions... a German... mhm... He questioned my intentions, mostly... I told him the truth, that I was a priest... no, I didn't mention the plan... yes... very well... *Bonsoir.*" Father Peter hung up. "I know you're standing there behind me," he said to Isidora, and slowly turned around to face her. She was halfway down the stairs. "You're far less subtle than a demon."

"I wasn't trying to be subtle," said Isidora, with a half-smile. "Why are you in Liverpool?"

"I suppose you wouldn't believe me if I told you it was for the old man."

He smiled back at her and looked her up and down as she descended the stairs. Her fragile frame contrasted with the strength of her personality. The lower level of the apartment was merely one small room where Stanley slept on a mattress. Father Peter hadn't bothered to turn on the lights, the flame of his cigarette preventing total darkness. She felt around for a light switch, but Father Peter gently took her delicate hand, and looked into her eyes.

"You're way more beautiful in the dark," Father Peter said. "I can see your soul so clearly."

"How rude," snapped Isidora, pulling her hand away. She found the switch and flicked on the lights. "The experiment! That's why you're here." Her smile grew wider.

"What gave it away?" Father Peter crossed his arms and took a step back, yet maintained an overconfident grin, while holding a cigarette between his lips.

"What other event could justify the Pope sending a priest with ridiculous abilities on an apparent mission to Liverpool? Mad scientist trying to create the afterlife."

Father Peter laughed. "Yes, the mad scientist caught the attention of His Holiness himself. I have a theory to test."

"I don't really care about your theory or what your reasons are," Isidora said. She paused and considered Father Peter's mission. She stepped toward him, took the cigarette out of his mouth, brought it to her lips and took a puff. "I want to sign up too."

Father Peter was getting sick of the sight of her in the light. She was so guarded, so difficult to read. He turned off the lights again and took his cigarette back. Her fear and fragility were drowned out by her screaming desperation. *Another Hell-bound soul grasping at any illusion of escape,* he thought. But, he did like the idea of being alone with Isidora in a virtual afterlife, however temporary it might be.

"All right," he said, moving closer to her, taking one of her hands, and bringing his other hand gently to her cheek. His thumb softly traced her thin, elegant lips, and he ran his fingers through her blonde hair, slowly moving his hand towards the back of her head.

"Oy!" Quentin ran down the stairs and turned on the lights.

Isidora slapped Father Peter across the face. Edward and Stanley watched from above at the top of the stairs. They'd all been eavesdropping during the entirety of Isidora and Father Peter's conversation.

"Not a bloody chance I'm going to Hell and seeing the ol' man again. I want in too!" said Quentin.

"And I want to go to the Exorcist Academy!" said Stanley. He threw a half-empty beer can down the stairs at Father Peter, hitting him on the cheek where Isidora had slapped him. The beer from the can sprayed Isidora in the face.

"All right, all right, fine!" said Father Peter, holding his cheek. "And I suppose you also have some kind of demand?" he asked Edward.

Edward hesitated. He hadn't thought of anything to ask for since he knew he was going to Heaven and didn't particularly want to be an exorcist. But since Father Peter had asked... "Ten thousand pounds," he demanded.

Father Peter groaned. "Fine. You two can come meet the team with me tomorrow. Stanley, I'll help you apply for admission to the Academy, and Edward, I'll give you..." Father Peter shoved a hand in his pocket, felt around for money, and pulled out what he could find, "–fifty dollars, as long as you all keep your mouths shut and stop hitting me."

They agreed to his conditions.

*   *   *

Father Peter, Isidora and Quentin sat across from Karl, Dalton, and Dr. Fanny Whalen. Darcy stood near the door, accompanied by Edward and Stanley, watching the meeting in progress.

"You're an odd group," said Dalton, looking at the three candidates distrustfully. Karl nudged him.

"They're heavily armed, too," said Darcy, almost in admiration, who felt powerful vibes emanating from the priest's tool box. With her trained soldier's eye, she'd also detected the outline of a switchblade in Quentin's pocket. Her remark was ignored.

"What my colleague Dr. McGovern here means is, it's very nice to meet you," said Karl.

"I'm sorry, would you mind if I just..." Dr. Whalen got up and placed her hands around Isidora's head. Isidora's eyes widened and she furrowed her eyebrows as Dr. Whalen felt around, pressing against her skull.

"Very nice!" said Dr. Whalen, and then looked toward Father Peter.

"Oh, my turn!" said the priest, smiling. He appreciated the view the head exam gave him of Dr. Whalen's cleavage.

When Dr. Whalen turned to Quentin, the menacing look in his eyes made her hesitate before approaching him.

"Dr. Whalen, please sit down," ordered Karl.

Dalton looked at Karl, shaking his head slightly. He then looked at Father Peter, Isidora, and Quentin and said, "Thank you for your time." He hoped they'd leave without causing too much trouble.

"Oh, come on now, they have the right energy!" Darcy said. "I have this feeling, like a déjà vu about this group. They're the ones!"

"Hang on," Dalton said to Father Peter. "You said your name was Father Peter?"

The priest nodded in agreement.

"Holy shit," said Karl. "What if he's—"

"The naked priest!" Darcy said, recognizing him.

"Sounds about right," said Father Peter. He winked at Darcy. She giggled, admiring his chiselled jawline.

"Well, now that we've established that Darcy's sense of déjà vu has nothing to do with your 'energies' but rather a simple coincidence, you may go," said Dalton, waving them away.

Karl looked at Isidora. She seemed oddly familiar.

"Are you by any chance a loss adjuster?" Karl asked.

"Used to be," said Isidora. She recognized him from a court case she was involved in some years back. "You're an insurance lawyer, aren't you?"

"Used to be," said Karl.

Edward looked closely at Karl, and his eyes lit up. "That's no insurance lawyer. That's Hitler!" he exclaimed, smiling and waving at Karl. "It's me, Eddie!" he said, as he shoved his way into the office. Edward bear-hugged Karl and rubbed his grubby hand through his hair. Karl winced. "You've grown out your hair! You looked harder with your head shaved. Can't see your skull tattoo anymore," Edward said, still rubbing Karl's head.

"Do you know this man?" Dalton asked.

"Not the slightest clue," said Karl, his voice cracking, partially from anxiety, partially because Edward's grasp was restricting his breathing.

"Ah, he's just messin' with you," Edward told Dalton.

Karl shook his head.

"Hitler's the best arms bloke in the civilized world!"

"I never asked to be called Hitler," Karl said to Dalton.

"So, you're Hitler the arms dealer," Quentin said to Karl. "It would be a shame if word got out to the police, or worse, to the associates you abandoned, who think you're dead."

"Surely there's some mistake," said Dalton. "Right?" He looked at Karl, who stared down at the floor.

"No, it's true," said Isidora, looking at Karl. "Just look at him.

The shame is obvious."

"I know exactly what you mean!" said Darcy. "Are you psychic too?"

"She's not psychic. She's just a bitch who says mean things to everyone. Me auntie doesn't realize some people have feelin's," Stanley complained to Darcy. Isidora felt her cheeks burn a little.

"My sister isn't psychic either," said Dalton. "She hadn't the slightest idea what Karl had been up to, or they wouldn't be living together," he said with assurance.

"I've always said I was a *little bit* psychic, not *a lot* psychic," Darcy argued. "It comes in flashes. Here I see a colour; there I see a light. But I don't see the whole picture, not yet anyway. I do feel I'm a bit more psychic than I used to be, especially since your..." Her voice trailed off as she looked at Dalton's face. He was biting his bottom lip, and Darcy knew it was a sign he was raging with suppressed anger.

"Suicide attempt," blurted Isidora, noticing Dalton's scars. His eyes widened and the room fell silent. Isidora's cheeks burned hotter.

Quentin stood up, pulled out his switchblade and flicked it open. "Here's what's gonna 'appen," he told Dalton, in a voice so low it was almost a growl. "You take us three for your little experiment, or Hitler's done pretendin' to live a lovely, normal little life, actin' all proper, workin' as a lawyer, shaggin' your sister."

"Oh, no, it's not like that," said Darcy.

Quentin ignored her protest. "Either we die, and go to your afterlife, or Hitler dies, an' goes to his." Quentin pointed his knife at Karl. His eyes were empty of any emotion or expression. "An' somethin' tells me he shouldn't be lookin' forward to it."

Father Peter nodded. "Hell-bound, sorry."

Dalton looked at Karl. He was breathing audible, short, sharp breaths. His hands were trembling slightly and his brow was covered in beads of sweat. While seeing Karl in terror was somewhat satisfying, Dalton didn't want him to die. He turned to Quentin and said with hostility, "Very well then, welcome to the team. You can make your appointments for surgery with Dr. Whalen."

The neurosurgeon clapped her hands and smiled brightly. *Cut, cut.*

"What an incredible series of coincidences," said Isidora. She looked at Darcy. "You had seen him before?" she asked, pointing to Father Peter.

"Did I ever," said Darcy with a wide grin, looking at Father Peter. He flashed her a smile.

"And the rest of us too, all seem to be connected in some way. Such an incredible series of coincidences."

"There are no coincidences," said Stanley, looking from Isidora to Father Peter. "Only fate."

Father Peter smiled and nodded to the boy approvingly. "You'll make a great recruit for the Academy." Stanley beamed.

Father Peter, Isidora and Quentin left with Dr. Whalen, followed by Edward and Stanley. Darcy, Karl and Dalton remained alone together in the office. Darcy took Dr. Whalen's seat.

"I think the boy is right," said Darcy. "It was meant to be."

"There's no such thing as meant to be," said Dalton. "We were coerced into taking them on as subjects because of Karl's recklessness," he said while glaring at his ex. "Seriously, Karl. You joined this team to protect us from potential liabilities when you were the biggest one of all. What are we supposed to do now? Give me one good reason why I shouldn't just turn you in to the police."

"Because you need me," said Karl.

Dalton frowned. "I don't need anyone. Now if you don't mind, I have a class to teach in fifteen minutes. Both of you, please, get out of my office."

CHAPTER SIX

Isidora lay down on the operating table. She clenched her fists reflexively, as if preparing for battle. "I've asked you before, but just to be sure... you put the thing in our heads, and then we just live out the rest of our lives normally, correct? Because I don't want to die just yet."

"Ideally, yes, however, there is a very high risk of complications. But the priest and the scary man are fine; they're in recovery," said Dr. Whalen.

The glaring surgical lights above Isidora illuminated the drab, grey operating room. She was surrounded by a team of medical professionals, led by Dr. Whalen. Her heart began to race when she noticed Dr. Whalen's blood-shot eyes—a tell-tale sign of a night of full-out partying without a wink of sleep. The anesthesiologist yawned. His hair was tousled, his eyes crusty. He pushed aside the medical student who had set up the IV in Isidora's arm and played around with it painfully. He leaned toward her and she caught a whiff of his morning breath and gagged a little. She watched the IV in her arm fill with general anaesthesia.

"No, no, this is all wrong, Sarah," the anesthesiologist told the medical student as he continued tugging at the IV. With those words echoing in her brain, Isidora went under.

*   *   *

"What is 'all wrong'? I'll sue you, I swear," threatened Isidora, upon waking up in the recovery room.

"Seven," said Quentin, from the bed to her left.

"What?" Isidora said, noticing the curtains on either side of her.

"That's the seventh time you've done that," said Father Peter from the bed to her right. "Pass out from all the drugs and wake up threatening everyone you'll sue them. You're starting to make Karl nervous. He keeps going on about how you can't sue them, that the agreement we signed is a flawless legal masterpiece."

"We're alive?" asked Isidora.

"Yes, we're fine," said Quentin. He sat up and pulled the IV out of his arm. "An' honestly, I don't feel like spendin' me next nights here with you people. See you in the afterlife!" He stepped out of bed and collapsed on the floor. Nurses rushed in, heaved him back into his bed, and attached restraints.

*   *   *

In addition to considering herself a little bit psychic, Darcy McGovern considered herself a little bit religious. Not enough to bother going to church every Sunday morning, but enough to follow the Pope on Twitter, wear a necklace with a golden cross around her neck, and visit the church when she needed to clear her head. Since the Florida trip, she avoided attending Mass since priests made her giggle at the thought of Father Peter, but she liked the paintings, as well as the peace and quiet that empty churches offered. She also believed the environment was good for developing her psychic abilities. She entered her favourite church and dipped two fingers in the holy water at the entrance of the church. She made the sign of the cross, bringing her fingers to her forehead, her chest, and to each shoulder. The water was cold, and she wondered whether it would be a sin to wipe it off her forehead. The smell of wood inside was calming. She took a deep breath as she sat on a bench, preparing herself for a mental conversation with God. Her eyes rested on a particularly bloody scene of Jesus being nailed to the cross.

"Hello, God, it's me again, Darcy McGovern," she said aloud

unintentionally. She looked around to see if anyone might have heard her. Reassured that she was alone, she carried on.

Hello, Darcy, she felt Him reply.

"I was wondering, do you think Dalton's experiment is a good idea? A lot of people seem upset about it. There are all those protests outside all the time, and there are all those movements to try and have the virtual afterlife banned. What do you think of all that?"

What do you think I would think of all that?

"I suppose you would think it's rubbish, that the afterlife is your thing, and that he shouldn't be trying to compete with you."

No one can compete with me. I'm literally almighty.

"You sound just like me brother. Anyway, I can't exactly tell him to stop, this project's the only thing that's kept him going since the incident, you know? It's nice he has a hobby. But it seems a little risky, playing with people's lives and afterlives. I'm not sure what to do about it, because I always try to be supportive of him. We never had it easy, Dalton and I."

Sorry about that.

"It's not your fault. Or maybe it is, but the Christian thing to do is to forgive, so I forgive you. At least Dalton and I have each other, and our health."

Not your mental health.

"Can't have it all. Anyhow, if there's anything I could do to help, without discouraging me brother too much, just send us a sign or something."

Thank you for letting me in.

"No, thank you. Have a nice day."

Darcy got up and left the church. She'd only started hearing God when she'd gotten her head injury, so in a way, she considered her fall down the coconut tree a blessing. This belief was strengthened when she'd met Father Peter—he who was at least in part the cause of her accident. *It was probably all part of some divine plan,* she thought to herself. This thought comforted her as she walked home.

*   *   *

"All right, you're free to go," Dalton told Quentin, Isidora and Father Peter, who were seated in front of his desk. "Enjoy the rest of your lives and I'll see you when you die. Unless you all outlive me, in which case someone else will be overseeing the experiment."

The three remained seated expectantly.

"Go along now!" Dalton waved them away.

"And what will you be doing?" asked Isidora.

"Oh, I'll keep developing the simulated reality. Presently it's more of a prototype, it looks a lot like the Albert Dock."

"That's exactly how Heaven is described in the Bible," said Father Peter.

"That's not possible. The Albert Dock didn't exist when the Bible was written," said Dalton.

Father Peter grinned. "Haven't you heard of the pilgrimage?"

"What, to the Albert Dock? No, there's no such thing," said Dalton, perplexed. *What an ignorant priest!* he thought.

Darcy walked into the room. "He's not serious, love," she said to Dalton. She sat down next to him and turned to the three subjects. "I thought it would be nice if we could all keep in touch. At the very least, exchange our contact information. I'd love to add you to my list of holiday card recipients. They're always good fun. Last year, a little reindeer was wearing an ugly Christmas jumper on the front and when you opened the card—"

Quentin got up and started to walk away. Isidora stood up, put her purse on her shoulder and followed him, but Father Peter stayed seated, his eyes glued on Darcy. He grinned broadly as she stopped mid-sentence. Her eyes rolled back, and she slammed Dalton's desk with both hands. Dalton fell from his chair, startled. Father Peter leaned forward in his chair, his eyes shining with excitement like a spectator at a championship football match.

"Defy my will, defy my command, and evil shall roam the Earth once more. Those led into temptation shall fall, and their souls shall be reclaimed. When the unnatural, the natural, and the supernatural become one, so begins the War of the Heavens."

Darcy lost consciousness, her head falling between her hands on the desk. Dalton gingerly tapped his sister's shoulder. She sprang up and was back to her usual self.

"You fuckin' twins give me the creeps," said Quentin, standing in the doorway. "I don't want your bloody demonic Christmas card." He left, slamming the door behind him.

"What's demonic about a reindeer in a jumper?" Darcy asked a horror-struck Isidora, who stood as if frozen in place for a moment and did not respond to Darcy's question. *Perhaps they don't celebrate Christmas*, Darcy thought.

Father Peter, though, was still seated in his chair, looking calm and even cheerful. "Nothing is wrong with a reindeer in a jumper, my dear. Whatever puts you in the spirit of the season," Father Peter told her. "I believe it's time for us to go, right, Izzy?"

Isidora took a few deep breaths as she regained the power of movement. "Don't call me that," she told the priest as she grabbed her purse and rushed out the door. Father Peter stood up and shook hands with Dalton and Darcy before leaving the room.

"They are an odd group," observed Darcy.

*   *   *

It was two p.m. in Vatican City and the Pope sat on his bed drinking red wine directly from the bottle with one hand and holding his iPad with the other. For the hundredth time, he was rewatching old videos from the sixties of former President of France Charles de Gaulle comparing Quebec's situation in Canada to Nazi-occupied France during the Second World War, and declaring Quebec's need for freedom.

"*Vive le Québec libre! Peut-être qu'on serait libre si les Québécois n'étaient pas une gang de lâches!*" the Pope yelled at the screen. He was about to throw the iPad to the wall when the screen went blank and then on it appeared a message from God. It made the Pope laugh. He got out of bed, dressed in his casual white outfit with the little round hat and went for a walk in the Vatican Gardens.

"Soon, we all die!" he told three Swiss guards as they crossed paths. They looked at each other, shrugged and carried on.

An Italian cardinal overheard the Pope's remark and pulled him aside, looking around to make sure no one would overhear their conversation.

"Your Holiness, do you mean the plan has come into effect?"

The Pope nodded. "It's all going to go down soon."

"And what about God's Paladin?"

"He will die any minute now." The Pope laughed.

"And he still doesn't know about the plan?"

"He knows about *a* plan. *The* plan... no, he doesn't. I gave him some bullshit plan that I wanted him to test some stupid theory of his."

The cardinal said nothing but avoided making eye contact with the Pope. It was clear to the Pope that the cardinal was uncomfortable with his decision to lie to Father Peter.

"Don't feel so weird about it. If Father Peter was not this smug bastard, he figure it out by now."

The cardinal sighed and nodded. "If it is your will, I trust it is for the best. Your Holiness... this is simply some friendly advice... perhaps a little more discretion would be a good idea."

The Pope laughed. "Sorry, I am drunk." He carried on with his walk and took out his phone.

*   *   *

Quentin was rather looking forward to seeing Edward and Stanley again. While he had been in hospital, they had been in Vatican City, completing all the necessary rituals and paperwork for Stanley's application to the Exorcist Academy. He had therefore heard very little of them during the past couple weeks. But they'd been back in Liverpool for three days now and he was surprised to feel a warm feeling in his heart at the prospect of their reunion.

He stood outside the front of the door of the flat, digging around in his pockets until he found his keys. There was a soft whimpering behind him and then something cold and hard pressed against the back of his head. A gun barrel. He raised his hands slowly, dropping his keys.

"A few years. A few years behind bars for murdering my husband," said a woman's voice. He stared ahead at the door.

"He deserved it, and I'd do it again," said Quentin. A bullet blasted through his skull and fragmented into several pieces inside his head. A piece of his brain flew back onto the widow and he collapsed to the ground. She looked at the bullet wound. A glowing red light emanated from inside Quentin's shattered skull.

*   *   *

Isidora struggled to keep pace with Father Peter as they left the university campus. "Tell me what you know," she demanded. Father Peter stopped. He smiled, reached toward her and brushed a wayward strand of hair from her face.

"You'll find out soon enough," he said. He flagged down a cab and got in, hurriedly closing the door before Isidora could join him. He waved to her as the cab left. She began to walk home, thinking of Darcy's perplexing outburst in Dalton's office, not noticing a bloodhound was following her.

Twisted version of the Lord's Prayer. Defy my will and the command of the Lord. I suppose I've done that. Temptation. Temptation to avoid the afterlife, most likely. I suppose it is all very unnatural.

Caught up in her train of thought, she failed to notice that two more bloodhounds were now on her trail.

Unnatural... so the unnatural is Dalton's experiment. The natural must be... well, normal life. And the supernatural... She thought of the old man. *They'll become one. What does that mean?*

She felt a sharp pain in both her shoulders and a crushing weight pushed her to the ground. She reflexively brought her arms forward, but they were gripped and pulled back before she hit the ground. As her nose hit the cement sidewalk, a crunching sound resonated in her ears. Hounds were at each of her arms, tearing off her flesh and gnawing into her exposed humerus bones. The gnawing and tearing in opposite directions made Isidora feel as though she were being hanged, drawn and quartered. The dog on her back had a paw on each of her shoulders and she could feel the heat of its breath behind her ear. It sank its teeth into the back of her neck.

*   *   *

Father Peter sat in the back of a cab, calmly waiting to die. He called the Pope. "Hello, Your Holiness. It's done. I should die any second now. All right. See you around."

"What the bloody hell is that supposed to mean?" asked the cab driver as they passed through an intersection.

"That," said Father Peter, pointing to a car that had just run a red light and was headed straight for the left side of the cab where Father Peter was seated. He shut his eyes and prayed for forgiveness. He felt pieces of metal and glass cut through his skin, lips, and eyes. He felt his jaw dislocate, and his teeth flew out of his mouth. His bones twisted and snapped in the most unnatural positions, severing his nerves and ligaments. His rib cage closed in on his lungs and his internal organs burst from the impact of the collision.

CHAPTER SEVEN

Isidora sat down on the wooden panels along the Albert Dock and took off her shoes. She dipped her feet into a surprisingly clear River Mersey, surrounded by the iron, brick and stone dock buildings and warehouses. Clyde approached her curiously. She held out her hand, and he hopped into it. She lifted him up and stroked him with her finger.

"Nice and sunny out, for once," said Father Peter. He rolled up his pant legs and sat down next to her.

"You died too, then?" she asked. Though her appearance was the same, her features had softened peacefully. Father Peter admired how the sun's reflection bounced off the water, into her eyes. *God is great. Wait, no. Dalton. Dalton is great?*

"You don't sound surprised," said Father Peter.

"The twin's prophecy. She said we would die for defying God. She was wrong about one thing, though." She gently reached for Father Peter's hand. "Dalton's experiment worked. We made it." She smiled.

Father Peter didn't want to say anything that would spoil the moment. "Yes, we did." He wondered if her lips were as soft as they looked.

Quentin ran over to them. "Look what I found!" Brooke the giant rat was cradled in his arms. Brooke was now the size of a large dog. Isidora ran away; the oversized rat reminded her of how she died.

*   *   *

"We're going to get sued. Worse, there are going to be criminal investigations. This is bad, Dalton. Very, very bad." Karl paced back and forth anxiously in the laboratory.

Dalton's eyes were glued to the screen, staring in awe. "I did it. They're all there. It worked. And I get to see it for myself."

"And your team did it with you!" Darcy added. "Well done, all of you!" None of the researchers acknowledged her. They whispered to one another, nodding. Slowly, they began to leave, one by one, and then in groups. "Oh, don't go! Don't you want to see how it all plays out?" asked Darcy. Only Dr. Fanny Whalen stayed back.

"I can't blame them for wanting to stay away from an inevitable murder investigation," said Karl. "How could they all die at once? Under such strange circumstances? One of them was definitely murdered, and it's not impossible the others were as well."

"The murderer shot herself after killing him. They know it's her. The others were unfortunate accidents. Now please relax and appreciate the miracle of my genius," said Dalton.

"Anyway, since when are you so concerned with crime?" Darcy asked Karl, teasingly rather than judgingly. Karl sat down next to Dalton and reached for his hand. Too absorbed in his experiment, Dalton ignored Karl's attempt at affection.

"I'm brilliant," said Dalton.

*   *   *

It had been an extraordinary year for young Stanley. Sometimes, he missed his mates from school. But his ma was annoying, and he never wanted to see her again. She was always telling him he didn't work hard enough in school, that he'd never achieve anything in life at this rate, that being the hardest lad around didn't mean anything past the age of sixteen. But then he met Quentin and Edward. They proved Ma wrong about everything. Being the hardest lad *did* mean something. You could spend your days at the pub, you could smoke whatever you want, drink whatever you want, do whatever you want, and no one could stop you. Stanley wanted to be just like them when he grew up.

Or, so he thought, until he and Edward opened the door to their flat and found Quentin lying dead on the ground. Stanley looked up at the widow. She turned the gun on herself, pulled the trigger and dropped dead. This made him particularly angry. How dare she kill herself before he had the chance to kill her? How he had wanted to kill her. He had his switchblade ready and everything. Now, Quentin was gone, and Stanley was beginning to wonder if Ma might have been right. Maybe Edward and Quentin weren't unstoppable just because they were the hardest men around. But Edward quickly talked Stanley out of that nonsense.

"No, Quentin's fine, he's just in a scientist's virtual world now," Edward explained to a tearful Stanley. "Now have another drink, and no. More. Cryin'," said Edward, reaching across the table to hand Stanley a beer.

"Liar," said Stanley. "When me pet chinchilla, Mr. Crabs, died, Ma told me he was livin' in Heaven now. But a week later, the neighbour's dogs dug him out of the backyard, and there were worms all over him and inside of him, eatin' his body."

"You gotta bury bodies good and deep if you don't want dogs digging 'em up," Edward commented. "But what the fuck kind of pet is a chinchilla anyway? They're only good for makin' posh coats. Should have got a big dog who can guard your stash for you," said Edward. "I used to have three bloodhounds. Good dogs, were they, real huntin' dogs. Sold 'em to pay a gamblin' debt."

Edward detected a tear rolling down Stanley's cheek, but pretended not to notice as the boy quickly wiped it away and hung his head. Edward handed Stanley a cigarette and clapped him hard on the back. "As for the worms eatin' yer furry rodent, you deserved to see that for namin' him Mr. Crabs. But for Quentin, death is different. It's not real death, it's something else. Something new."

Stanley lifted his head and asked, "What is it?"

"I'm not exactly sure, but we can find out. Let's go to the lab."

*   *   *

Isidora sat inside an old, darkened warehouse, her back pressed against the cold brick wall. It was completely empty; Dalton hadn't gotten around to creating anything inside the buildings yet. All at once, the lights came on. Quentin walked in.

"I'm sorry about the rat," he said. "I thought it was funny." He sat next to her.

"My reaction was irrational," she said.

"You know, we don't have to sit on the ground," said Quentin. "Watch this." His eyes filled with intensity as he scanned the room.

Red carpeting with floral patterns began spreading across the floor, and the red brick walls transformed to an elegant white with golden mouldings. Isidora gasped as a rose and golden sofa appeared. Quentin nudged her shoulder and pointed to a mahogany desk and chair. Out of nowhere, he held a bouquet of pink and white roses in his hand and gave them to her.

She felt herself blush. "Thank you."

"Save your thanks—that's just the beginning." He pointed to a golden grand piano that emerged in the centre of the room. An enormous crystal chandelier hung above it. She raised her eyebrows as Greek statues of black marble further adorned the room. In the middle of the west wall, a great white fireplace flickered with pink embers and plumes of purple smoke.

She sniffed deeply. "How lovely, it smells like lavender."

Quentin smirked and nodded. Next to the fireplace grew a glorious Christmas tree decorated in gilded glass balls and flashing silver lights.

"My goodness," she said. "This is where the Queen gives her Christmas address."

Quentin nodded. "We can make loads of things happen in here just by thinking about them. I thought this room suited you. You remind me of the Royals."

Isidora suspected the entire spectacle was a beautiful and elaborate insult. Regardless, she would make the most of it. She sat down at the piano and played a joyful Beethoven sonata. He sat on the sofa and listened. When she finished, he clapped ironically.

"Well done!" said Quentin. "When you grew up you were rich enough for piano lessons. You must be very proud! How about a bow, Milady?" He joined her by the piano, tore the chandelier from the ceiling and smashed it against the floor. He ran over to the Christmas tree and began launching the fragile balls forcefully against the walls, laughing maniacally. They shattered into several pieces, like the bullet in his head. He paused.

"Are you satisfied now?" asked Isidora, sitting at the piano, her arms crossed.

"No." He pulled the tree down, nearly hitting Isidora. He grabbed more balls and kept throwing them. "Have I offended Her Majesty?"

Isidora got up, walked over to Quentin, and picked up a Christmas ball. She crushed it in her hand. His eyebrows raised slightly.

"No blood," she observed, looking at her palm and letting pieces of glass fall to the ground. "We can't be hurt." She reached for her pocket and found her cigarette lighter. She set the Christmas tree on fire.

"We can't be hurt," repeated Quentin.

She grabbed him and kissed him.

*   *   *

Father Peter sat by the docks with Brooke and Clyde. Brooke was frustrated she couldn't eat Clyde; she would bite him, feel the satisfaction of sinking her teeth though his body, look down, and see him still standing there, perplexed as she chewed on thin air. It was most confusing for the oversized rodent.

Father Peter pictured his tool box and it appeared next to him. He pulled out a few candles and they lit on their own. He set them up, closed his eyes and prayed.

"In the name of the Father, the Son and the Holy Ghost," he said, making the sign of the cross. "Your Holiness, can you hear me?"

The Pope's voice resonated in his mind. "What you want?" asked the Pope.

"I'm in the virtual world. It seems all very intact. It may even be impenetrable."

"Have some faith, you smug bastard," said the Pope. "God is telling me there is a design flaw. Apparently, the computer shit can be destroyed from the inside. He will need your help."

"What can I do?" asked Father Peter.

"There will be a sign. When you see it, you will know what to do."

The candles went out. *Typical God, always so mysterious,* thought Father Peter, who took a deep breath. It smelled of burning. Father Peter opened his eyes. A warehouse went up in flames, the fire rising to the virtual blue sky. The smoke spread across the River Mersey. *Smoke on the water,* he laughed. He pictured a turntable and it appeared and played the Deep Purple hit. *Could there be some kind of significance to this? Smoke on the water. Smoke. Holy smokes. Holy smoke. Holy smoke on the water. Holy water. This whole world is almost entirely water. If I bless the water, it will all be God's.*

*   *   *

"What a load of rubbish," said Stanley, staring at the blank screen in the laboratory. He threw a can of beer at it. It hit the screen and drenched it in beer.

"They really are in there," insisted Dalton. "There's a function I've programmed, which enables them to blank out the screen if they don't want to be seen doing something. Apparently, at the moment, the three of them are up to something they don't want us to see. But they're there, I promise."

"Liar!" Stanley kicked Dalton in the shin and stomped on his foot. "You're just as bad as me ma and the chinchilla!" he said, punching Dalton in the stomach repeatedly. "Now someone give me a ciggy before I get angry!" He reached for his switchblade.

Darcy strode up to Stanley and boxed his ears. "That's unacceptable be'aviour from a little boy. You should show more respect, me brother was nice enough to let you in here." She let him go. He wiped a tear from his eye and sat down.

"No fuckin' cryin'," Edward said to Stanley. "You're going to let a girl hit you and make you cry?"

Darcy marched over to Edward, boxed his ears as well and shoved him into a seat. "Now all of you, sit and be patient," she said. "They'll show up. It's their afterlives; they can do what they like."

*　　　　　*　　　　　*

Chief Constable Evelyn Glasgow stood before her team. After three years leading the Merseyside Police, she still felt an adrenalin rush bordering on a panic attack when public speaking was required of her.

"It's no secret strange things have been going on here for some time," she told her officers. "And it all started when this man came back to Liverpool." She pointed to a picture she'd found on Facebook of Karl, posted three years ago on a beach in Marseille, holding up a pink cocktail, his shirt unbuttoned, showing off his juvenile build. Below the picture she had written *Karl Schmidt, aka "Hitler"*.

"He's a psychopath and a master manipulator. His suspected crimes in France and Morocco have still gone unpunished. You know how the French are, surrenderin' all the time."

"Fuck the French," said a ginger policeman.

"Jokes aside, he's very good at covering his tracks. We know what he does, but we can't quite pin anything on him. However, the moment he came back to Liverpool, this lad, Stanley Wexler, went missin'." She pointed to an unfortunate school picture of Stanley blinking halfway, mouth half-open. "And this all coincides with Quentin Campbell's release from prison last year. I know I don't have to show you a photo of Campbell. You know him all too well."

"What does the lad have to do with the German and the murderer?" asked another policeman with black hair and a short, greying beard. He remembered shamefully how he inadvertently threw out most of the evidence against Quentin Campbell in his murder investigation, mistaking it for rubbish. Campbell got off easy because of him. But since that fiasco, he'd given up drinking and proven himself a rather efficient member of the police force.

The Chief Constable felt her white shirt collar and black tie tighten around her neck as her heart raced. She had difficulty controlling her rapid breathing. "At first glance, you wouldn't think there's a link. Until you bring him into the equation." She pointed to a picture of Dalton in a brown trench coat. He was cosplaying the tenth Doctor at a convention, pointing a sonic screwdriver at the camera man, wearing 3D glasses. It was the only picture of him they could find online. Despite his growing name recognition due to his controversial experiment, Dalton never accepted to be filmed or photographed and was unaware he was featured on Instagram on a cosplay account.

"Dr. Dalton McGovern and Mr. Schmidt first became lovers while studying together at Oxford."

"Ha! Gay," said the ginger policeman. The Chief Constable glared in his direction, took a deep breath and carried on with her presentation.

"After Oxford, Schmidt followed McGovern to Liverpool. They lived together for four years and then Schmidt left for France, before venturing to Africa and the Middle East."

"Did the other one go to Middle Earth?" asked the bearded policeman, in reference to Dalton's apparent interest in imaginary worlds. The joke earned him a few laughs. Evelyn Glasgow's heart raced, she counted down from ten, exhaled slowly, and continued her presentation. She resisted the urge to inform him that he was confusing Tolkien's Lord of the Rings with Doctor Who, because she knew that if she did, they would laugh at her and she would likely faint from the humiliation.

"Ever since Schmidt came back for McGovern, it seems all hell has broken loose in Liverpool. Most recently, Peter Nightingale, or 'Father Peter,' came to Liverpool." She pointed to a picture of Father Peter at a strip club in Montréal, Québec, surrounded by topless women. "He's an international drug mule who poses as an exorcist for the Vatican, of all things.

"Nightingale and Campbell were both subjects in Dr. McGovern's experiment. The third subject was this woman, Isidora Prentice."

She pointed to a picture of teenage Isidora at a music festival, surrounded by her friends, wearing white denim mini shorts and a black bra. She was covered in glitter. "Prentice was arrested a couple times in her youth for drug-related charges. But the most striking connection to this case is that she is Wexler's aunt."

"Lucky boy," said the ginger policeman, who'd moved up closer to get a better look at Isidora's photo.

"Not really. The three subjects died under mysterious circumstances at the same time, and it is likely that Stanley Wexler is dead as well."

"What's this all mean?" asked the bearded policeman.

"Here's my theory." Chief Constable Glasgow adjusted a contact lens in her hazel eye. It was beginning to itch. She needed to blink more often. "Schmidt and Campbell are connected through a mutual friend, Edward Reid. Reid and Campbell were living together after Campbell's release from prison. Reid and Campbell are both part of a street gang that, among other enterprises, supplies illegal arms to the UK. Reid and Schmidt worked together directly in the past. When Schmidt decided to return to Liverpool, he reached out to Reid, who integrated him into his group and introduced him to Campbell.

"Nightingale was likely a drug mule known to the group, and Prentice, a client. Prentice was probably bored with her life, getting fired from her dull, dead-end job as a loss adjuster after an exciting youth. Drugs were the only thing that kept her going. She'd even returned to the pub she worked at when she was younger, an establishment known for hosting a great deal of criminal activity. When Prentice was behind on payments, they punished her by abducting, and perhaps murdering, her nephew, Wexler. As for McGovern, he didn't welcome Schmidt back like he'd hoped. Proof is Schmidt lives with McGovern's twin sister, Darcy McGovern, a veteran. She was discharged after getting shot in the head, the poor woman."

"A hero," said the ginger policeman.

"Dr. McGovern was having difficulty finding anyone for his experiment, so in an attempt to win him back, Schmidt got a few acquaintances to volunteer. What Schmidt didn't tell him was that he would have them all murdered so Dr. McGovern could witness for himself his experiment's success. A hit-and-run killed Peter Nightingale, likely one of Schmidt's hitmen. Campbell appears to have been murdered by the widow of his victim, however, it seems awfully convenient she turned the gun on herself immediately after. As for Prentice, she was torn apart by a pack of dogs once owned by Edward Reid and, at the time of the attack on Prentice, were owned by another member of the gang. Uncoincidentally, the gang in question has been linked to a secret dog fighting league active throughout the north of the United Kingdom. I would even suggest that Reid himself is a trainer of assassin dogs."

"You say uncoincidentally, but what if these events are just a big coincidence?" asked the bearded policeman.

The Chief Constable felt her racing heart pound against her chest once more. She took a few deep breaths.

"There are no coincidences. My theory? Karl Schmidt is a psychopath in love, desperately trying to bring back that spark between him and Dr. Dalton McGovern, no matter the cost. Since his return to Liverpool, Schmidt has been responsible for the murder of three, if not four, individuals. Your mission is to find whatever evidence you can linking him to the murders and the kidnapping. Schmidt has killed, and he will kill again."

*　　　　*　　　　*

Father Peter had never blessed such a large body of water. He tried a few typical prayers, but nothing happened. The water was still very much virtual. For a large body of water like the River Mersey, he'd have to bring out the old Latin.

"*Exorcizo te, creatura aquœ, in nomine Dei Patris omnipotentis, et in nomine Jesu Christi, Filii ejus Domini nostri, et in virtute Spiritus Sancti,*" he began. He skipped a pebble across the water. It bounced three times and sank under water. Disappointing. He continued.

"*Ut fias aqua exorcizata ad effugandam omnem potestatem inimici, et ipsum inimicum eradicare et explantare valeas cum angelis suis apostaticis, per virtutem ejusdem Domini nostri Jesu Christi: qui venturus est judicare vivos et mortuos et sœculum per ignem."* He skipped another pebble. It bounced six times. Better. Unfortunately, it still only travelled in a straight line. But faith began to fill his heart.

"*Deus, qui ad salutem humani generis maxima quœque sacramenta in aquarum substantia condidisti: adesto propitius invocationibus nostris, et elemento huic, multimodis purificationibus prœparato, virtutem tuœ benedictionis infunde; ut creatura tua, mysteriis tuis serviens, ad abigendos dœmones morbosque pellendos divinœ gratiœ sumat effectum."* He skipped another pebble. It reached the other end of the square dock and circled back like a boomerang. He picked it up. Nearly there.

"*Ut quidquid in domibus vel in locis fidelium hœc unda resperserit careat omni immunditia, liberetur a noxa. Non illic resideat spiritus pestilens, non aura corrumpens: discedant omnes insidiœ latentis inimici."* He skipped the rock again. It circled about the square of the dock in a figure eight formation. God's infinite power.

"*Et si quid est quod aut incolumitati habitantium invidet aut quieti, aspersione hujus aquœ effugiat: ut salubritas, per invocationem sancti tui nominis expetita, ab omnibus sit impugnationibus defensa."* He tossed Clyde and Brooke into the water. They stayed under for a few minutes and rose out of the water, levitating a couple feet in the air. The rats' dull grey fur now shone of silver and Brooke had shrunk to her previous, God-given size. Cleansed of all sins. He grabbed them out of the air and put them down on the dock.

"*Per Dominum, amen."* He dove gracefully into the water, feeling the sins wash right off him. It reminded him of a magic mushroom trip. He felt connected and united with the forces of nature, led only by intuition and faith in God toward a greater understanding of universal truth. He came out looking exactly the same. After all, he was already perfect looking, in his opinion. Without even having to enter a meditative state, he contacted the Pope.

"You again?" asked the Pope.

"Your Holiness, I did it. God has entered the virtual world. The barrier between the virtual world and the Heavens is broken."

"Don't expect praise for doing your job. Only expect punishment if you fuck everything up. Now find a demon and see how the exorcism goes. Report back to me when you're done."

"How am I supposed to find a demon in this holiest of virtual worlds?"

"Figure it out."

*   *   *

Quentin lay topless on the ash-covered floor, his hands behind his head. Isidora rested her head on his chest and traced his prison tattoos across his body with her finger. She was attempting to wish them away with her mind with the help of her newfound abilities in the virtual world, but they wouldn't go away. Quentin must have been attached to them for some odd reason, but she couldn't bear to look at such mediocre art. She sat up, buttoned her blouse and fixed her hair.

"Sex in a fire, that's a first," Quentin said.

Isidora stood up and started toward the door. Quentin ran up to her and grabbed her from behind just before she went outside, sliding his hands up her blouse.

"There's no reason to feel guilty," he said. "We're dead, who's judgin'? Nothin' wrong with enjoyin' ourselves. We can do whatever we want, whenever we want." He unhooked her bra and kissed her neck. "Whatever we desire." He reached around her and unbuttoned her blouse. She smiled and leaned back into his arms. With him behind her, she didn't have to look at his tattoos.

"Do you hear that?" asked Isidora, turning to the piano. It was playing Rachmaninoff's prelude in C# minor on its own. "Are you doing that? You think that's funny?" She pulled away from him, buttoned her blouse up once more and ran over to the piano.

"It's not me, I swear," he said. "Izzy, back away from the piano."

"Don't call me Izzy."

A sulphurous fog-like being began to form in front of her. Grey hands floated over the piano; long fingers with thick yellow nails gently pressed down on the keys. From there appeared a pair of skeletal arms, a body, and a head, with long, stringy white and grey hair, visible only from the back. Isidora approached the figure.

"Isidora, don't," said Quentin, placing a hand on her shoulder. She gently pushed him back and took a step closer. She reached a hand out.

"Isidora, please—"

The figure's head turned back 180 degrees. It was the old man.

"Missed me?" he asked.

Quentin grabbed Isidora's hand and pulled her away. They ran out of the building, the old man racing behind them.

"Where is Father Peter?" asked Isidora.

*   *   *

Dalton considered it a rotten deal, having to teach introductory linear algebra in exchange for giving the university the privilege of being home to the world's greatest scientific achievement. Nonetheless, he obliged, and was admittedly enjoying the admiration of his keener students. Many showed up early to his evening class, hoping to get a seat at the front. Others stayed behind after class to chat. Accompanied by a slide show, Dalton gave his presentation before the auditorium.

"Last week, we went over the concept of an echelon matrix. Can anyone tell me the difference between the row echelon form and the reduced row echelon form?"

The students in the front row raised their hands at once. A student in the back pulled a slice of pizza directly out of his bag and took a bite. The students sitting along the sides tried to blend in with the walls to avoid being called upon. Dalton pointed to a young man with straight dark hair in the front.

"Yes, Stephen."

"You remembered my name," said Stephen.

"I remember everything."

Avoiding eye contact with Stephen, Dalton inadvertently looked into the projector, which briefly blinded him. He blinked as his eyes watered.

Stephen's time had come to impress Dr. McGovern.

"When a matrix is in row echelon form, the leading entry is 1, each leading entry is in a column to the right of the leading entry in the previous row, and rows with all zero elements are below rows—"

"Dalton!" Darcy ran into the classroom. "Your bloody experiment's gone mad, and you left me and Karl alone in there with Edward and the child! None of your bloody researchers have come back yet. There's only Dr. Whalen, who is just as clueless as us about computers."

"Did you try turning it off and back on again?" Stephen suggested.

Dalton pulled Darcy aside. "You're making me look like an amateur in front of my class," he whispered, avoiding his students' curious eyes.

"Well, I don't bloody care how it looks. What looks bad is all the funny business written on the screen."

In that moment, Darcy saw in Dalton's eyes something she'd never seen before. It resembled fear combined with confusion. Incomprehension. "What does it say?" he asked.

"It's written in red, 'Possible intrusion detected,' across the screen, flashing." Darcy held up her fists to his face and then flicked out her fingers. She repeated this gesture over and over, imitating the blinking message.

"That's not possible. No one could get past my firewall."

"How could I make up something I don't even understand? We're all panicking in there: Karl's already preparing various legal defences, Dr. Whalen can barely hold the child back from destroying your servers, and Edward broke into the vending machine in the hallway and he's stealin' all the snacks. What's the bloody message about?"

"That's the IDS."

"The what now?"

"The Intrusion Detection System."

Dalton addressed the classroom. "Class is dismissed. Someone has hacked the afterlife."

CHAPTER EIGHT

The Albert Dock provides a significant geographic advantage in favour of non-demonic beings when the River Mersey is filled with Holy Water. Isidora and Quentin, followed by the old man, raced towards Father Peter, who was lying flat on his back on the wooden deck by the water.

When he caught a glimpse of the river, the old man screeched at the sight of the overwhelming quantity of holy water and stopped in his tracks. Quentin and Isidora carried on until they reached the priest, whose eyes were shut behind his sunglasses as he gloried in his latest holy accomplishment.

"Father Peter!" Isidora got on her knees and shook him by the shoulders. "The old man is back!"

"Don't be so hysterical," said Father Peter. He yawned and slowly sat up.

He lifted his sunglasses and looked up, squinting. The old man stood behind them on the concrete, unwilling to go down onto the wooden deck by the water.

The old man cackled. "Father Peter, we meet again."

Holes in the old man's head, chest and hip appeared where Father Peter had shot him during the exorcism. Green fluid oozed out of the holes, as well as his eyes, nose and mouth. It leaked down onto the deck where the three were sitting. As the substance spread over the deck, the wood began to disintegrate.

"Oh, that's awesome!" Father Peter said to Quentin and Isidora. "Just what I needed, a demon!"

Isidora imagined the old man inside a cage. A metallic box formed around him.

"How did he get in the virtual afterlife?" asked Quentin, grabbing Father Peter by the collar and shaking him aggressively.

"I have no clue," said Father Peter. He laughed, and Quentin punched him in the nose.

Father Peter grinned. "You can't hurt me here, Quentin."

"Oh, you bet I can," he said. "Guess what Isidora and I were up to just before the old man came back?"

Isidora elbowed Quentin and nudged him out of the way.

"What were you doing earlier?" she asked Father Peter.

"Praying, enjoying the sun..." he laughed.

There was a sizzling sound; the old man's green fluid was beginning to burn through the walls of his cage. Isidora fixed it.

"There's something different about you," she said to the priest. "What are you hiding?"

Quentin pointed to the new and improved Clyde and Brooke. "Look at the rats! He did somethin' to them. I've been tryin' to make the big one big again, and I can't."

"And you won't," said Father Peter. "Now release the demon. I want to try something."

"Not until you tell us what's going on," said Isidora. "You said you sent the old man to Hell. Why is he here?"

Father Peter sighed in resignation. "Let's ask the Pope." He gestured for the three to sit with him, cross-legged, holding hands.

"*Encore toé esti?*" asked the Pope. "Make it quick."

"Your Holiness, there's a demon here in the virtual world. The old man from Liverpool."

"Perfect. Kill it and tell me how it goes, whether it is different, more easier than usual, like you theorize in your report."

"Your Holiness, I'm just trying to understand how this is possible. I blessed this world. How did a demon get in?"

The Pope grunted. "*Criss de cave.* What you did is bless some water. All that means is you broke the barrier between the supernatural world and the unnatural world by letting God in.

God, demon, whatever. Anyone can get in there if they feel like it now."

Father Peter, Isidora and Quentin all looked at each other, panicked. The old man cackled again, more loudly this time.

"Your Holiness, you said I would be bringing God into this world. You never said I would be bringing in demons."

"You're so naïve, Father Peter," said the old man. "You really think He tells you everything He's up to?"

Quentin imagined duct tape over the old man's lips, who mumbled and failed to cackle again.

"Father Peter, you are an exorcist. Your job is to kill demons, not to ask all these questions. *Criss-moi patience.* Goodbye." The Pope left the conversation.

The old man ripped the tape off his mouth. "Silly Father Peter blindly following orders. You think you're so rebellious, don't you, with those impure thoughts about Icy Isidora over there."

Quentin laughed. "Icy Isidora! Good one."

The old man's voice began to echo inside Father Peter's mind. "You could be great, you know. All that power, all that potential, wasted as a pawn in His game. Cast aside by the church, like a freak! Hidden in the Academy as a boy, trained to hate your own strength. Sheltered from the outside world, deprived of any authority, robbed of any free will, forced to live the gruesome, violent, lonely life of an exorcist."

Father Peter placed his hands over his ears and screamed in agony, his blood burning through his veins. He grabbed a knife from his toolbox and cut his hand. Instead of blood, he watched the demonic green fluid flow out. He fell to the ground.

"Get out of my head!" he cried, clutching his bleeding hand, tossing and turning.

"What's the matter with him?" asked Quentin. He looked over. The old man was still in his cage.

Isidora bent down and gently ran her fingers through Father Peter's hair. She held his hand, which looked perfectly fine to her. He pulled it away.

"Don't touch me, you slut!" he said in a hoarse, unrecognizable voice. He screamed in pain and laughed simultaneously, his eyes rolling back and his body twitching and twisting unnaturally.

"Yes, she's a nasty one," said the old man. "So suspicious, so distrustful... always asking questions, never giving answers. She should be punished. Punish her, Father Peter. You're so weak, such a penetrable mind, from all that repression. Imagine how strong you could be on our side. When the war begins, you're the kind of leader we will need. Punish her!"

"She doesn't deserve it," said Father Peter between agonizing breaths. "She can still be saved."

The old man chortled. "Save her until the next time she spreads her legs open for a Hell-bound creature. Go ahead, Father. Look at him."

In Father Peter's mind, the whites of Quentin's eyes were bloodshot and his irises transformed from brown to red. His skin shed off in flakes, revealing a new layer which appeared burned beyond the third degree, cracking and bleeding the green fluid with every motion. Quentin's voice was so hoarse Father Peter could hardly understand the words he hissed to him: *Father Peter. Father Peter.*

"Father Peter!" said Quentin. "Are you all righ'? Can you hear me?"

Father Peter jumped at Quentin's throat, strangling him. The old man laughed.

"How is this possible? How are you hurting him here?" asked Isidora.

"My tool kit! Give it to me so I can kill this demon!" said Father Peter in terror. Quentin tried to push him off, but was incapable of hurting him back.

Isidora opened the toolbox. She took out Father Peter's sharpened cross and sprinted to the old man's cage.

"What are you doing?" cried out Father Peter. "Isidora, give me the cross. I have to kill Quentin!"

Isidora took a deep breath.

One...

She tightened her grip around the cross.

Two...

She raised the sharp end in the air at the old man's eye level.

Three.

The cage disappeared and she swung for the old man's head. His icy hand grabbed her wrist and she felt as though her bones would be crushed from the pressure of his grip. She dropped the cross. He pushed her to the ground and lay face to face with her, gripping both her wrists. He smiled and opened his mouth unnaturally wide, breathing his frigid, misty, sulphurous breath into her face, stopping her from breathing. The green fluid projected out of his mouth onto her face. Isidora felt as though acid burned through her skin.

*   *   *

Dalton typed furiously on his keyboard. He was surrounded by Darcy, Karl, Stanley, Edward and Dr. Whalen, all watching the screen in vain.

"I've never seen malware like this before," he said. "What I'm about to say will sound mad, but it's almost like it's... sentient."

"It is," said Darcy. "You've tapped into something you shouldn't have. Went where you had no business going. If you could just—" Darcy's expression went blank and her eyes rolled back. She placed a firm hand on Dalton's shoulder. "Unnatural Defiler, your reign is over."

"That's homophobic," said Karl.

"Your world is Mine and the final barrier will fall, releasing My soldiers, and *his*, into the natural world. The War of the Heavens has come. Witnesses, decide for which side you shall fight. Defiler, you have made your choice."

Darcy lost consciousness and fell, hitting her head against the floor. Dr. Whalen sprang into action, kneeling by Darcy.

"Everyone, step back," ordered Dr. Whalen. "No one touch her nor try to move her, she may have a spinal injury. Karl, call an ambulance. Edward, get Stanley out of here. Dalton, keep working on the program. Something tells me it's of utmost importance you keep to it."

Edward and Stanley made their way to the door. "Stan, I think it's time to take you back to your ma's. We've had a good run."

Stanley stopped in front of the door and crossed his arms. "I want to say goodbye to Quentin. You promised I would see him." His eyes welled up with tears.

"I'm sorry, Stan. It's all fucked."

Edward considered hugging him to console him, but decided against it. He didn't want Stan to go soft. He scratched his beard and opened the door to find himself face to face with Chief Constable Glasgow, accompanied by six policemen. He slammed the door shut. He and Stanley leaned against the door as she pounded on it with her fist.

"Karl Schmidt! I know you're in there," shouted the Chief Constable.

Karl was on the phone, describing Darcy's accident to the operator.

"He's busy," said Stanley. "So, fuck off."

The door burst open, knocking Edward and Stanley to the floor. The bearded policeman reached for Stanley, who dashed to the back of the laboratory, fairly swiftly, despite his limp.

"Stanley Wexler! You don't have to be afraid anymore," said the policeman. He approached the boy slowly with his hands out, palms up.

"I told you it would be a mess in here," whispered Chief Constable Glasgow to the ginger policeman. "Karl Schmidt, you're under arrest for the murders of Quentin Campbell, Isidora Prentice, and Peter Nightingale, and for the kidnapping of Stanley Wexler."

Trying to finish his conversation on the phone, Karl waved away the ginger policemen approaching him.

"Are you resisting arrest?" said the ginger. He grabbed the phone out of Karl's hands and tossed it on the floor. He pulled Karl's arms back and cuffed him.

"I was calling an ambulance! Can you not see the unconscious woman on the floor?" asked Karl. The ginger kneed him in the stomach.

"What did you do to her, you sick freak?" demanded the ginger.

"Nothing!"

The ginger kneed him again, this time in the sternum. Karl felt a rib crack and he exhaled sharply.

"He's being very insubordinate," the ginger told his colleagues. The other policemen rushed towards Karl, some stepping over Darcy's body.

"All of you, get out of the way!" shouted Dr. Whalen. Her cry got the attention of Chief Constable Glasgow, whose focus turned from Karl to Darcy. She rushed to her unconscious body to assist Dr. Whalen.

"What happened here?" asked the Chief Constable.

"She fell and hit her head," Dr. Whalen said. "She could die if she doesn't get immediate medical attention. I'm a neurosurgeon, you can take my word for it."

"I'll call an ambulance right away. Your name?" asked the Chief Constable.

"Fanny. Fanny Whalen."

While the Chief Constable called for an ambulance, Edward rushed over to the five policemen who were now taking their turns hitting Karl. Edward punched one in the nose, but another officer grabbed Edward from behind and put him in a chokehold. While the policemen were distracted by Edward, Karl kicked the ginger in the groin.

Stanley limped away from the bearded policeman, who followed him at a slow pace, wishing not to intimidate the child. Stanley stopped and reached into his pocket. He gripped his switchblade.

"You're okay, lad. It's time to go home now," said the bearded policeman.

Stanley nodded. The bearded policeman held out his hand. Stanley flicked open his switchblade, cut the bearded policeman's hand and took off to assist Edward and Karl. He stabbed aimlessly into the melee.

Dalton stood up on a chair, his back turned against the large, blank screen.

"Everyone, listen to me!" he commanded.

The chaos continued. Paramedics burst in to assist Darcy.

"That's enough! Everyone, get out of my laboratory!"

The room went silent. The lights flickered. A crippling sense of fear filled the hearts of all those present in the laboratory. The paramedics and the policemen ran out of the room. The others slowly backed away from Dalton.

"Thank you for your cooperation." Dalton smiled. Clearly, teaching university classes had allowed him to develop his leadership skills, he thought.

"Excuse me, Mr. Scientist," said Stanley in a small, meek voice. "Did you write that on the screen?"

Dalton turned around. His hands trembled.

"No, I did not."

On the screen was written, *Go ahead, Dalton. Defy me.*

The words disappeared and were immediately replaced with a new message.

Evelyn Glasgow, do you still feel clever?

The Chief Constable looked around the room. "What's the meaning of this?" Her voice quivered. No trick nor breathing technique could counteract the cortisol, norepinephrine and adrenalin flooding her sympathetic nervous system.

Despite all the rational justifications running through people's minds, every single person in the room had an underlying feeling that the truth was something far beyond their comprehension. The laboratory went cold and seemed crowded, though eerily quiet.

Edward Reid, you're like a desperate old dog that needs to be shot right between the eyes, the screen read.

Edward couldn't find it in him to make a witty remark about the message. No defence mechanism could overcome the unsettling disconnection he felt from reality.

Hitler, how are those handcuffs treating you? You should know, the police left with the key.

Karl felt the handcuffs tightening around his wrists. Panicking, he tried to pull his arms apart. The cuffs tightened even more.

Perhaps Stanley and his switchblade could help. It can't cut through metal, but with some determination, it can cut through flesh.

Stanley put his knife back in his pocket. He felt too numb to cry.

Poor good-hearted Darcy. It would be a shame if she didn't pull through.

The lights flickered.

To make matters worse, something most unfortunate is about to happen to Dr. Whalen.

The lights went out.

"Where is Dr. Whalen?" asked the Chief Constable, noticing she was now alone with Darcy.

The servers hummed and vibrated increasingly, then stopped at once. A violent silence filled the laboratory. The screen shattered. Behind the screen was a dark, empty, eternal void.

"I've seen this before," said Dalton. "This is where people go when they die."

"Dr. Whalen, what have you got in your hand?" asked the Chief Constable.

All eyes turned to Dr. Whalen. It was a wire saw, an instrument designed to cut through skull bones.

The lights flickered again, revealing that Dr. Whalen's eyes had turned yellow. A blank expression on her face was slowly replaced by an unnaturally wide smile.

"Cut, cut!" she said.

She lined the wire up against her forehead and dragged it from right to left repeatedly, cutting through her skin. A stream of blood poured down from her forehead, into her eyes and over her grin, colouring her lips and teeth red. As she cut through her skull, the sawing resonated like nails on a chalkboard combined with cracking and popping sounds as the bones snapped from the pressure, echoing in the otherwise silent laboratory. She reached her prefrontal cortex, and blood now flowed from her head down to her toes, her white lab coat now completely reddened. She persisted to cut through her brain until she collapsed upon reaching the motor cortex. The top of her head flopped open, exposing her severed brain.

While an overwhelming urge to scream filled the lungs of everyone in the room, an instinct froze them, not unlike that of a spider crawling up a wall who's been spotted by the person intending to crush it and flush it down the toilet.

Karl's eyes shifted toward the windows. The moon shone oddly red in the night sky, illuminating the laboratory. The lights flickered on and Karl caught a glimpse of a figure in the window's reflection, standing behind Dalton. It vanished when the lights flickered off, and when they came back on, the figure appeared slightly closer to Dalton.

"Dalton, don't turn around. Just look at me. But there's something behind you."

Dalton felt a presence, as if someone were peering over his shoulder. The chair shook as Dalton's knees weakened.

"What on Earth could it possibly be?" Dalton muttered, not daring to speak fully aloud. The lights turned off.

"Funny choice of words," said Karl. "I have this creeping suspicion we're not in the realm of 'Earth' anymore." The lights flashed on. The figure was immediately behind Dalton.

The lights went out. A chill crept down Dalton's spine, slowly, as though a cold fingernail were tracing down each of his vertebrae. His chest tightened. His feet felt like two cement bricks, stranding him on the chair.

The lights flickered on. "I think you should get down from the chair and start walking towards me, and away from... him," said Karl.

The lights went out. "Who is *he*?"

The lights flickered on. "Looks a bit like... an old man."

The lights went out. Dalton felt a cold wind that smelled of sulphur brush up against his left cheek and was vaguely aware of a dark figure in his peripheral vision. His eyes shifted ever so slightly to the left, and they met the gaze of two empty white eyes only half an inch from his face. His instincts finally kicked in, and he prepared to dart away with the full power of his adrenalin. But a freezing, misty hand with jagged fingernails gripped his shoulder. The old man opened his pitch-black mouth, revealing his carnivorous, brown, rotting teeth while emitting a piercing cry.

And then Dalton saw nothing.

CHAPTER NINE

Isidora screamed as the green fluid burned her face. She frantically wiped her eyes and cheeks in an attempt to get the acidic venom off her skin, but couldn't seem to get rid of the pain. She felt something cold drag across her face, followed by a sense of relief.

"Holy water from the River Mersey," said Father Peter, wiping her with a white hand towel.

She opened her eyes and they met his. They were joyful as ever.

"Is the old man gone?" she asked.

"He's gone."

"Thank God you're all right," she said, and threw her arms around him.

"Great choice of words," said Father Peter.

"Thank God *he's* all right? He attacked me!" said Quentin, pushing Father Peter aside. "And none of us is all right. Look at the bloody sky!"

The bright blue sky was growing increasingly pixelated, like a low-resolution image. The buildings and the river followed, fading into a series of coloured dots outlined in black. The three looked at one another and realized that they themselves were becoming pixelated. The colours of the world around them were reduced to various fluorescent shades of red, green and blue. Any distinction between the sky, the warehouses and the people blended into a series of pixels. The number of pixels increased exponentially, until they appeared completely black. Isidora, Father Peter and Quentin found themselves inside a dark void of non-existence.

"No wonder the old man took off," said Quentin.

"Are you all still there?" asked Isidora. Though nothing was visible, nor audible, she could feel their presence and hear their thoughts echo in her mind.

"You say that as if it were possible for a soul to disappear," said Father Peter.

"What a rubbish afterlife," said Quentin.

"If the old man got out, so can we," said Isidora.

The empty, seemingly eternal void was oddly claustrophobic.

"It's important not to get lost in here, so try to keep it together," said Father Peter, though it was unclear whether the advice was for the others or for himself.

Isidora gathered her wits. She visualized how the world used to be.

"Father Peter, the old man got into the virtual world because you blessed the water, correct?"

She felt his confirmation. Concentrating and visualizing the lost world, Father Peter sensed the image she was recreating. He added himself to the image, standing over where he blessed the water.

"The barrier broke in the River Mersey," she said. "But how do we retrace that in here?" She stopped visualizing, snapping back to the reality of endless darkness.

"Based on the pattern of the pixels, and relying on your mental picture, I've managed to map it out," said Quentin. He felt Father Peter's astonishment and Isidora's skepticism.

The truth was, Quentin loved maps, graphs, charts, and any visual representation of organized data. But he especially loved maps. His fondest childhood memories included boxing, football, studying the topography of southeast Asia, creating a 3D map of the London Underground, discovering Canada through its federal electoral results per constituency over the years, travelling through America by memorizing the routes of the country's major highways, and learning about Spain's regions by analyzing their climatic variations. He considered himself a successful cartographer; he'd made quite a bit of money drawing out maps of prisons with details of their inner workings and selling them to inmates wishing to escape. They were annotated with recommendations on different breakout strategies, assessing their risk levels.

Above all, star maps were Quentin's favourite. Historically, these grids allowed navigators to discover new worlds using the stars as their sole points of reference. Without the stars to guide them, sailors upon the vast oceans would have surely felt trapped in an eternal void of non-existence until they finally reached land at the end of a maddening journey.

Dalton was no astronomer nor geographer. Constellations were not replicated in his afterlife. And there was something off about the Albert Dock. As the world pixelated away into nothingness, Quentin observed a logical, orderly pattern in which Dalton had carefully placed each building, each wooden panel, each inch of concrete and each cloud in the sky. It greatly simplified interpolation for Quentin. The sun was the upper limit of the afterlife, which Quentin somewhat arbitrarily assigned a value of +100 on the Y axis measuring height, for simplicity's sake. The bottom of the River Mersey hardly respected nature, but rather Dalton's own pleasure in symmetry. -100 on the Y axis. The Dock formed a perfect square around a part of the River Mersey, stretching on the X axis of length and Z axis of depth. The centre of the square was point 0 on all three dimensions. Point 0 was the heart of the afterlife and it was likely where the barrier was broken following Father Peter's ritual.

Quentin recalled that after Isidora had been sprayed by the old man, the ghost had vanished. Father Peter had come back to his senses and had brought Isidora back onto the deck along the water. The three of them were therefore on the water level when the world disappeared.

"We have to head in a straight line that way," said Quentin. Isidora and Father Peter found "that way" to be a rather unclear instruction in the void.

"Go on then, get in me head so you can see me map. It's not so bad in here." He could feel Father Peter and Isidora's reluctance to enter into his mind, like it would taint their souls. But they were out of options.

Entering Quentin's mindspace was hardly the angry, harsh and impulsive environment they had imagined. Rather, it was rational and calculating. On the level of the water, he had created a perfect epitrochoid which mapped out the shape of the afterlife on a flat surface. Based on the formations of the clouds, Quentin had created a grid, which enabled him to establish the distance between different points in space. He transposed the grid onto their level to adequately measure the distance between themselves and point 0.

"Why... How..." started Father Peter, failing to decide which of the many questions running through his mind he should ask.

"The scientist is a real bloody madman, creating a world this bloody symmetrical. It's unnatural, the whole thing," said Quentin.

"He used Clyde!" said Isidora. "I recognize this pattern. Dr. McGovern intended to create more to the afterlife. Just like Father Peter, he did something to Clyde, altered his personality and his abilities—probably by changing his code, certainly not by tossing him into holy water. The radius of the epitrochoid follows the pattern by which Clyde would burrow and swim about. The radius grew ever so slightly each time Clyde made his rounds, extending the delimitations of the virtual reality. Brooke was likely programmed to do the same, and she was bigger, more efficient."

Isidora thought of Father Peter's strange rodent baptism. "But you ruined it all. Whatever you did to the water, to the rats, you changed Dalton's code, likely because of the abilities within your own code. Our power over our environment was too great and you somehow managed to destroy the structure of the virtual world."

"It was God's will," said Father Peter, defensively.

"Who gives a fuck about any of that," said Quentin. "Let's get the bloody hell out of here. Follow me map."

The three made their way to point zero. It was difficult to say whether they travelled in a nanosecond or a year; in the void, time seems to stand still while simultaneously accelerating. It gave Quentin motion sickness. Yet when they reached point zero, they found themselves in Dalton's laboratory.

*   *   *

Stephen the student had few followers on social media. He wasn't an attractive fellow, nor a particularly sociable one. He liked to tell himself that none of that mattered because he was clever, but the truth was, he wasn't. Stephen was a man of only little talent. However, for the first time since he broke his personal record playing Mario Kart in June, Stephen was treated with a wonderful dopamine hit. Like. Retweet. Like. Retweet. Stephen's post had gone viral. #HackTheAfterlife was trending on Twitter. *Thank God I recorded Dr. McGovern's discussion with his sister in class. Perhaps now I will finally get a girlfriend. Or at least a female Twitter follower,* he thought. Alas, his most recent follower was not at all a potential girlfriend, but rather Pope Clement XV.

The Pope read the Tweet while he groomed his docile, though opinionated, caramel-coloured Shih Tzu, Sébastien. Combing the dog's fur with one hand, he scrolled through tweets with the other. *Enfin, tabarnak,* he thought. The moment he'd been waiting for throughout his entire career in the Catholic Church had come. He called a meeting with the Church's elite cardinals in the Vatican's underground wine cellar. He brought Sébastien.

The cellar had been modelled off the catacombs in Paris, only the walls were lined with French wines, not French skulls. Sébastien liked sweet white wine from the Alsace region. The Pope preferred red wine. Sébastien deplored this preference.

Three cardinals approached the Pope, wearing dark red cloaks. Their hoods were pulled up over their foreheads, leaving only their wrinkled mouths visible. The Pope wondered how they didn't trip more often considering their compromised vision.

"Your Holiness, for what reason have you summoned us?" inquired an Italian cardinal.

"It work. The virtual afterlife explode everywhere," said the Pope. The cardinals looked at one another, confused, and looked back at the Pope. Once again, the Pope found himself having to explain everything to old cardinals who weren't on Twitter. "The barriers are breaking between the unnatural, the natural, and the supernatural. Angels and demons will wander around and soon, the apocalypse is going to be starting."

The cardinals nodded.

"Has the void begun to expand, yet?" asked a cardinal from Mexico.

The Pope shook his head. "I believe, for now, it is still contained just in the laboratory in Liverpool. There is probably a dozen demons in there now, either coming out and possessing people or lurking in some corners and wherever, waiting for the war to start. I will fly into Liverpool myself tonight."

A cardinal from Spain cleared his throat. "Your Holiness, what about the exorcist?"

"He is still thinking I just want him to test his theories in his bullshit report. He doesn't know about the apocalypse."

"Has he figured out who he is?" asked a cardinal from Italy.

"He doesn't know none of this. It will stay like that," replied the Pope.

The meeting ended, and the Pope left Sébastien in the Mexican cardinal's care. The cardinals scooped up as many bottles of wine as they could hide under their cloaks and entered the Vatican's secret elevator, only known to the Pope, a handful of cardinals and Sébastien. Before the door shut, the Spanish cardinal shouted, "God's Paladin shall be victorious!"

The Pope glared but ignored this declaration. He wasn't going to let some radical cardinal ruin his day.

Shortly after, the Pope boarded a flight to Liverpool, on which he enjoyed a variety of snacks and beverages. He watched the impeccably dressed flight attendants walk up and down the aisles in their high-heel shoes. *How do they keep their hair that nice and shiny?* he wondered.

Passengers whispered to one another and pointed in his direction. He smiled and waved at them. Some people came over to tell him it was an honour to meet the leader of their faith, and others came over to tell him how much they liked his tweets. Many were astonished to see the Pope flying economy on a commercial flight, but he never liked to make a fuss about his travels. For one thing, he judged luxurious travel to be a terrible use of offering-payer dollars. In addition, the Pope believed that it was his duty to engage with the people, not to stay locked away in the Vatican like some princess trapped in a hexed palace, giving the odd speech from his balcony. He enjoyed meeting people, it reminded him why he spent so much time trying to save their souls in the first place. Sure, his odds of being assassinated were greater, but that was almost ideal, since his death would be epic and forever remembered. However, an even better death awaited him than assassination: an apocalyptic death. The best way to be remembered forever is to be the last Pope of all, the Pope who valiantly led God's soldiers in the War of the Heavens.

*   *   *

Stanley slowly brought his index finger to his lips, informing Father Peter, Isidora and Quentin to remain quiet. However, this gesture informed Dalton, who had his back turned to them, of their arrival. He stepped down from the chair and turned around.

"I'm glad you found your way out," said Dalton, grinning. His eyes were empty.

"What's wrong with him?" asked Isidora.

"The old man's in him," replied Edward.

Dalton walked toward Isidora, who crossed her arms.

"You should see your reflection," said Dalton. "Your inner beauty is shining through."

Dalton pulled back a lock of her hair. She hit his arm away.

"Auntie Isidora, what happened to your face?" Stanley asked.

Isidora brought her hands to her cheeks and realized she'd lost all sensation in her face. Her skin had a thick texture. She turned to Father Peter, hoping for an explanation.

"You're a bit pink," said Father Peter.

"You look like all the skin on your face was peeled off," Quentin clarified.

"You don't look so good yourself," said Isidora.

Quentin's brown eyes seemed to grow dimmer by the minute, and his skin began falling off in flakes.

"Well, you look absolutely gorgeous," said Chief Constable Evelyn Glasgow to Father Peter.

He flashed her a smile. Father Peter's eyes shone brighter than ever.

"The thing is, we're dead," said Father Peter. "Our souls are transitioning to their true form."

Isidora fell to the floor, screaming in agony, as her skin blistered across her body. The pain felt similar to the green substance the old man had sprayed on her face. Dalton cackled.

"Hurts, doesn't it? Hell fire," he said.

Dalton looked at Quentin. His skin was peeling off gradually. Quentin's face showed no emotion.

"You're always so stoic, so hard. You feel nothing, do you? No remorse... what a good soldier you'll make," said Dalton. He looked at Quentin's clenched fists. "Oh, are we in a bit of pain?"

Quentin's uppercut reached Dalton's nose and knocked him unconscious. Edward and Stanley cheered. Karl ran over to Dalton and knelt by him, his hands still cuffed behind his back. Every time he took a breath, he felt like he was being stabbed in the chest from the rib the ginger broke when he'd kneed him.

"That's not your mate, that's the old man," Quentin said to Karl.

"Actually, it's also Dr. McGovern," said Father Peter. "When someone is possessed, their soul shares their body with the demon. It's a bit like having a shitty roommate."

Quentin shrugged. "He deserves it for ruinin' the experiment."

*   *   *

Isidora screamed in agony. She felt her eyes fry and her heart burn from the boiling blood it pumped through her body. *If only there were some way out of this,* she thought. She looked at unconscious Dalton, and then Darcy, who both lay on the floor, motionless. What if it were possible to visit people's minds like she could in the void?

"*This one's mine,*" said the old man, as she tried to visit Dalton. "*Quite something, this mind of his. Sometimes he has a bit too much fun with knives, cutting his wrists... his sister has had to bear the weight of it,*" he continued. "*Go ahead, Isidora. Try it. It's good fun.*"

The old man sent an image into Isidora's mind. It was Dalton's suicide attempt. She watched Darcy rush to his rescue. *Perhaps that could be a way of luring her in*, thought Isidora.

"*Yes, try it*," said the old man. "*Her mind is so weak right now, can't you feel it? It's so easy to play tricks on a failing mind. Why not ask our friend over there for help?*"

Isidora looked at Dr. Whalen's dead body. The neurosurgeon's severed head turn toward her. Dr. Whalen grinned, winked, and her head dropped dead on the floor once more. Isidora saw through Dr. Whalen and felt another entity occupying her body.

Darcy sat up with a gasp. "Dalton!" she cried, looking at Dr. Whalen's body. The Chief Constable wrapped her arm around Darcy, trying to calm her down. Darcy pushed her aside.

Where Dr. Whalen had last stood, Darcy thought she saw Dalton, holding a razor to his wrists. "Put it down, love," Darcy said, shaking her head.

The Chief Constable followed Darcy's gaze, perplexed. "Who are you talking to? There's no one there, only Dr. Whalen's corpse."

Darcy ignored the Chief Constable. Her eyes were glued to her hallucination of her brother. "It's all right, Dalton, I can help you. Just give me the razor." She slowly reached out her hand.

The Chief Constable looked around the room. Dalton still lay unconscious, across the laboratory. "Whatever it is you're seeing, it's not your brother," she told Darcy.

Darcy stepped towards what she thought was Dalton, and he cut open his wrists, blood flowing out forcefully and drenching the entire laboratory, spattering across the walls and spreading along the floor. She watched Dalton fall and saw his body lying on the floor where Dr. Whalen's corpse truly lay.

"Not again," said Darcy, her heart racing. She tried to make her way toward the spot where she believed him to be, but the Chief Constable pulled her back.

"Don't go there," said the Chief Constable. "There's something... bad... over there."

"Let me go! I have to help him!" Darcy cried, struggling against her.

"What are you talking about? That's Dr. Whalen's body."

Still holding her back, the Chief Constable tried to keep Darcy away, but Darcy pulled them both closer to the body. Darcy turned to face the Chief Constable and shoved her in the chest, trying to break free. The Chief Constable resisted, and Darcy pulled harder toward the body, dragging the two of them down to the floor alongside Dr. Whalen's corpse.

Thank you, said the entity inside Dr. Whalen to Isidora. The entity entered Chief Constable Glasgow's mind while Isidora's attention turned to Darcy.

Darcy grabbed Dr. Whalen's arm, believing it was Dalton's.

"Someone, help me, please," said Darcy, looking around the room. She felt faint, her head pounded, and the flickering lights of the laboratory overwhelmed her. She thought she might be concussed again.

She looked at Karl beseechingly. He knelt by Dalton's actual unconscious body. Darcy, upon seeing Dalton over by Karl, became aware of the stiffness of the arm in her hands, looked at it and realized it was not her brother's, but Dr. Whalen's, tensing up as rigor mortis set in. She dropped it in horror. Darcy heard Isidora's voice inside her mind.

"*I'm terribly sorry,*" said Isidora to Darcy. "*The pain was unbearable.*"

No, no, I haven't had an episode in over a year, thought Darcy. She began braiding her hair with shaking hands. "Focus on the braids," she told herself, controlling her breathing. Isidora searched Darcy's mind, looking through memories of Afghanistan.

Lying on the floor, her wicked soul streaming into Darcy's mind more and more, Isidora felt like something hit her from behind. She became overwhelmed with an urge to kill Karl. A voice inside her own mind—not the old man's, but another one, more authoritative, spoke to her.

"*We'll need all the numbers we can get for the upcoming war,*" said the voice. "*Karl is one of ours. Get her to kill him so he can join us. But don't get her killed. She'll join them.*"

Dalton sat up and ignored Karl, who had been kneeling by him with his hands still cuffed behind his back. Through empty eyes, he stared at Stanley. "Finally, I can punish you properly," he said.

Dalton grinned and slowly made his way over to the boy. Karl thought of following him, but noticed Darcy staring at him, braiding her hair.

"Darcy, are you okay?" asked Karl. Her eyes were glued to him.

"*Don't you remember, Darcy?*" Isidora told him. "*You're United Kingdom Special Forces. He's an enemy of the Crown. Supplied weapons to terrorists across the northern hemisphere. You're on a mission to kill him.*" Isidora played with the memories in Darcy's mind, altering them at her will. It startled her to see naked Father Peter in there.

Darcy stared blankly at Karl. She'd finished braiding her hair, and her arms dropped suddenly. He struggled to move toward her, still on his knees.

"How's your head? How are you feeling?" he asked. He was now just a few feet away from her and could see that her pupils were not evenly dilated. She glared and took a few steps towards him.

Karl tried to get up on his feet, but Darcy pushed him back down. She stomped on his shin, which snapped in half. Karl cried, feeling the bone rip through his skin and press up against his skinny jeans, which became soaked in blood around the wound.

Despite sharing Darcy's mindspace, Isidora still lay on the floor, her body hardly recognizable from all the blisters. She cackled.

"*Yes! Do it!*" she ordered Darcy, her voice raspy. Father Peter looked at Darcy and turned to Isidora.

"Isidora, I know a part of you is still in there," he said to her. He bent down and gently touched her shoulder. It burned his hand, and he pulled it away.

Father Peter's voice drew Isidora out of Darcy's mind and made her once again aware of the pain she felt. "I can't bear it," she said weakly. "I can't stand the pain. I have no choice." She tried to focus on Darcy's mind, but Father Peter kept speaking to her, splitting her mind between herself and Darcy.

"There's no escaping your own soul," said Father Peter. "You can leave, take over innocent people's minds, but when you do so, you lose control."

"That's not true," said Isidora. "I can be free from this pain if I want. Why should she get to have that body all to herself, when souls like mine suffer? I want to be free of this pain."

Father Peter pulled out the cloth he'd soaked in holy water from his toolbox. It was still a bit damp. He pressed it against Isidora's cheek. She winced, looked briefly relieved, but then screamed and convulsed.

"You aren't free. If you accept Hell, you accept to be under the reign of a False God. That's how he lures you in. He makes you believe sin is freedom. But sin leads to a greater loss of control, and to greater suffering. You become his pawn, and your suffering will be endless. He's doing this to you to control you, to use you. Fight back!"

Isidora cried and struggled to form sentences in spite of the pain of her bleeding vocal cords. "I can't. It's where I belong."

"It's not too late for you, Isidora," said Father Peter. She was surprised to find comfort in hearing her own name. "There is marvellous grace in redemption, and eternal love in salvation."

Between convulsions, Isidora managed to whisper a few words. "It's too late. It's too late."

Father Peter held her hand, despite it burning his own. "So long as you're here, it's not. Hang on, and fight."

CHAPTER TEN

Edward had been in a perpetual state of confusion since the day he picked up Quentin from prison. Life was already confusing enough before. He had no idea what taxes were for so he didn't pay them; he never opened his mail; he failed to understand why there was a Prime Minister if there was already a Queen who ruled the world with her lizard friends; and he didn't know why the Americans wanted to blow up the moon. But life became far more confusing when the old man, the angry child, the cowboy priest, the sexy aunt and the mad scientist showed up. Edward wondered if maybe the government was putting something in his water to mess with his head, and that none of it was real. Or perhaps it was the new strain of cannabis he'd been smoking, which was laced with a powerful hallucinogen. He considered the former scenario to be the likeliest. Drug dealers were far more trustworthy than governments. Maybe governments were the true drug dealers, and drug dealers were actually secret governments. Maybe they were the lizard people. There were so many possibilities; *how can a bloke keep 'em all straight?* he wondered. Despite his various theories, Edward knew deep down that none of the changes in his life were drug-induced hallucinations.

Edward stood face to face with Chief Constable Glasgow. He never liked bizzies, but he especially didn't like the look of this one.

From behind, she looked fairly attractive despite her uniform. She had very small feet. He liked that in a woman. However, he found her particularly unappealing when she turned her head back to look at him and cracked her neck unnaturally far over her shoulder. Her eyes were yellow, like a snake. *Because all bizzies are snakes.* He laughed at this thought. He'd owned many snakes in the past because he enjoyed feeding them mice. However, his laughter stopped suddenly, and he felt like he was going to throw up his own heart from fear when the Chief Constable darted toward him with Dr. Whalen's wire-saw. It dawned on him that if she were the snake, he was the mouse. She was awfully bloody fast, that bizzy.

She lunged at Edward and pinned him to the floor. She pressed the wire-saw up against his neck and tried to force it downwards as he held her back by her forearms. She managed to cut through the surface of his skin. He resisted and nearly pushed her off when she leaned down, sank her teeth into his cheek and bit off a piece of flesh. Edward felt that the teeth on the side on his mouth were now exposed to the cool air of the laboratory. He bled from his cheek into his mouth, and he wondered if he might drown on his own blood. The Chief Constable spat out the piece of cheek she'd bitten off, and Edward seized the opportunity to push her off of him while her head was turned away. He took the wire-saw out of her hands and threw it aside. He felt bad at the idea of hitting a woman but decided that in this particular case it was justified. He punched her in the head, which smacked her skull against the floor. A small amount of blood trickled down from her nose and out of her mouth. He wasn't quite sure if she was unconscious or dead. It was all very confusing.

*   *   *

Stanley scuttled towards the door, away from Dalton. He seized the knob and turned it as hard as he could, but it wouldn't budge. He slammed his body against the door, hoping to force it open. Still, it did not move.

"The door swings the other way, you stupid, foolish child," said

Dalton. Stanley turned to face him and flicked open his switchblade.

"Back off, ol' man," he yelled, holding up the blade.

Dalton leered, clutched Stanley's arm and grabbed the blade out of his hand. He rolled up his own shirt sleeves, studied the scars from his suicide attempt, and traced them with the switchblade, lightly cutting through his skin.

Stanley's knees began to tremble and he sank a little against the door. Dalton laughed and turned the knife on the boy, holding it against the bridge of his nose.

"Which eye do you like best? I'll start with your least favourite if you behave."

Dalton traced Stanley's undereye circles with the blade, scratching the delicate skin deep enough to draw blood. Stanley began to cry, and his tears blended with the blood, turning his teardrops red. Stanley tried his usual tricks, shin-kicking, elbowing, even karate chops, but nothing seemed to bother Dalton. Instead, he grinned. His teeth were sharp and rotten, like the old man's. Even the skin on his face was beginning to decompose.

"Answer me, lad," insisted Dalton, as he brought the tip of the knife up to the white of his right eyeball and pressed lightly. Stanley wailed. Dalton cackled.

Father Peter raced over to Dalton's side, brandishing his crucifix.

"Release Dr. McGovern now, old man," commanded Father Peter.

Dalton slowly turned to face Father Peter. He chuckled and put Stanley in a chokehold.

"You'll have to kill the child to get to me," he said.

Father Peter decided he would put his theory about exorcisms to test. He was dead, and that came with some newfound abilities. He entered Dalton's mind.

What he found there reminded him of the void—mostly empty space. However, unlike the void, binary code floated about. The thoughts in Dalton's mindspace made Father Peter feel like he could never love again, never laugh again, that all he was capable of feeling was resentment, cynicism, and contempt. He spited everyone for their joy. *How dare they smile in such an indifferent world? How dare they rub it in my face that they are blissful in their stupidity? How dare our society reward them for their dullness? How dare we admire their basic desires and ambitions and applaud them for reaching the most primitive and underwhelming milestones a person can achieve? How dare they overlook my genius and pity my loneliness?*

Father Peter felt so angry. He was torn between wanting to destroy himself and wanting to prove himself better than everyone else. Did the world deserve him? Should the world know how much better he was than them all?

Father Peter heard the old man's voice echo inside Dalton's mind. "Funny, is it not? What an unpleasant little man. I bet having me as his mind's main occupant is an improvement."

"Definitely not," said Father Peter. "This is a troubled soul, but it can be saved."

Father Peter searched for the old man inside Dalton's mind. Where would a demon hide? In his emotions? In his memories?

"Dalton," called out Father Peter. "Can you hear me?"

The old man kept talking. "He's gone. This is all mine now. You're wasting your time, and Stanley's starting to wonder what's going on with you."

Father Peter became aware of a distant call. He made out the words; it was his own name.

"Father Peter, do something!"

Father Peter left Dalton's mind and came back to reality. Dalton still held the knife to the child's face, but kept tormenting him instead of cutting him.

"Bad children must be punished!" Dalton shouted, but the boy's two eyes were still intact.

Dalton is stopping him, thought Father Peter. *He's still in there.* Father Peter noticed Dalton's bloody forearms and realized that the cuts traced over his scars, reminding Father Peter that Dalton had tried to kill himself. It was likely his most painful memory. A great place for a demon to torture his soul. Father Peter re-entered Dalton's mind.

He walked through the void and observed the binary code surrounding him. Father Peter suspected Dalton was so uncomfortable with his own emotions and memories that he had to break them down into the least human form possible; a series of ones and zeros.

"Dalton, you're going to have to show me how you feel. Somehow. Just clue me in."

Father Peter waited. Nothing.

"I just need a sign. Anything. You can't keep it all locked away forever, or the old man will win."

"He doesn't trust you," said the old man. "He doesn't like the way you think. It's not compatible with his mind. You can't get through to him."

Father Peter ran around aimlessly, looking for a sign from Dalton's soul. But there was nothing.

A gentle voice spoke to Father Peter. "Luckily, great minds think alike."

Father Peter looked toward the sound of the melodic voice. Isidora stood next to him, with a half-smile. Father Peter shook his head.

"Isidora, you have to get out of here. If you drift from your soul much longer, you'll be lost forever and tortured for all eternity. Please, go back, and fight."

Isidora shrugged. "This is my mess. Had I not let Stanley leave my home, none of this would have happened to him. I don't have any fight left in me, but if I can get rid of the old man, I can free Stanley. And besides, Dalton doesn't like you. There's more of a chance he'd like me."

"Why would anyone like you more than me?" scoffed Father Peter.

"Because I... get him."

Isidora opened her arms, raised her hands and looked around, showing Father Peter the evolution of Dalton's code. It had gone from binary to abstract words, among other symbols and numbers.

"Now, where would a demon hide?" she asked.

"In his most painful memory."

"His suicide attempt," Isidora said with a nod. "All right, Dalton, I'm not a programmer. Show me something I can work with."

The code evolved from somewhat coherent phrases describing various commands, to full length sentences.

"He's describing what he's done ever since the old man took over," said Father Peter.

"Over there," said Isidora. "The old man cut Dalton's wrists where he had originally cut them himself."

The code became increasingly abstract until it was in binaries again.

"What a load of rubbish," said Father Peter.

"No, it's not," said Isidora. "He gave us a clue."

Isidora repeated the series of 0s and 1s to herself continuously, with an inhuman ability to retain numbers.

"His actual suicide attempt would only be slightly different. The action is the same, but the depth is greater. With this code, we will be able to find where in his mind he has stored his suicide attempt," said Isidora.

Father Peter reached for her hand. "I'm worried about you," he said. "These abilities of yours are reaching far beyond your normal capacities."

Isidora smiled. "I suppose being dead allows me to think outside the box."

Inside the code-filled void of Dalton's mind, walls, staircases, and corridors began to form.

CHAPTER ELEVEN

Chief Constable Evelyn Glasgow died and the entity found itself trapped in yet another corpse. It scanned the room for weak minds it could easily penetrate and realized Isidora had vacated Darcy's. It entered Darcy.

Hello, little bitch, it said. Darcy stood over Karl, in a haze. *Aren't you a violent one! We're going to have to put those killing skills to use today.*

Darcy's eyes became yellow. Karl, wheezing, tried to push himself away from Darcy using his one good leg. Darcy looked down at him and smiled.

"Someone's been up to no good," she said.

"My apologies," said Karl in a choked voice. Beads of sweat, as well as tears, ran down his face from the pain in his leg and chest, the fear of greater pain and imminent death, and the helplessness of having his hands cuffed behind him.

Darcy looked back and smiled at Edward.

"Eddie," she said politely. "I was wondering if you could do me a favour," she asked. She cracked her neck from side to side.

Edward nodded, because opening his mouth to speak would have been far too painful given his recent mauling.

"Could you give me the wire-saw next to you? I would like to take Karl's handcuffs off and I'm sure it would cut through steel."

Edward looked at Karl. He shook his head. Edward turned to

Darcy. He generally thought she was a lovely young woman, almost as kind as his nana, though something seemed off today. He picked up the wire-saw and walked over to them.

Edward held up the wire-saw to Karl and Darcy, pointed to it, pointed to himself, and finally to Karl, hoping it was clear he intended to cut the handcuffs off himself. Something told him he shouldn't give the wire-saw to Darcy like she'd asked. He bent down and took Karl's wrists.

"We have to get away from her, quickly!" whispered Karl, which caused him a great deal of physical pain in his chest. He watched Darcy grab a chair and raise it over Edward's head.

"Behind you!" shouted Karl.

Edward turned and was hit face-first with the chair. Darcy beat Edward repeatedly until his head was an unrecognizable pile of flesh, bone and blood. Karl tried to push himself back with his one good leg as he was sprayed with blood from the attack on Edward. Darcy took the wire-saw out of Edward's lifeless hand and walked over to Karl. She grinned.

*   *   *

Quentin sat in a corner, his arms wrapped around his knees. His head rested back against the wall. He tried to focus, resisting the urge to acknowledge the excruciating pain burning through his entire body. The more he gave in, the worse it got.

Compared to Isidora, he looked rather well. Though his skin looked more like scales and his eyes were dim and bloodshot, he was still recognizable.

I'm not going to burn in Hell, thought Quentin. *That wasn't the deal. The deal was I get to be in a computer program forever. I'm going to stay that way. I'm not going to burn in Hell. I'm sick of being a prisoner.*

He tuned out the chaos around him and within him. He tried to think of ways to keep his mind occupied.

There once was a girl named Izzy,
Who I fucked to keep me'self busy,

She went through point zero
And wants to play hero
But burns herself into a tizzy

There once was a priest named Pete,
Who fucked everyone he would meet,
He shot an old man
To help little Stan
But fell for the old man's deceit

There once was a man named Hitler
Who fucked his ex-boyfriend's sister,
He sold us a gun
Said thanks for the fun,
And went back to being a barrister

There once was a man named Quentin,
Who had just gotten out of prison,
Then a scientist said
You'll wish you were dead
When I'm done with your mind and your skin...

Quentin looked at his skin. It dried up and cracked with every movement he made. He bled the acidic green substance. He shut his eyes and went back to his limericks.

*   *   *

Father Peter watched Isidora analyze the code in Dalton's mind, and followed her as she raced through a maze of digits and symbols. She was as beautiful as ever, though something seemed different about her. He felt her humanity fading away as her supernatural ability to understand the intricacies of Dalton's mind patterns increased. He thought of reaching for her hand, but he felt he'd only get in the way of her investigatory delight. He felt somewhat useless, following her lead, until he recognized a hauntingly familiar melody.

"Isidora, do you hear that?" he asked.

"Rachmaninoff's prelude in C# minor!" she said. "Let's follow it."

"But it's coming from everywhere, Izzy. The old man is taunting us."

"Then we must be getting close."

He followed her until they reached a dark, narrow corridor lined with steel doors on either side. She stopped, and Father Peter caught up to her.

"This is it," said Isidora. "Where Dalton has stored all his memories related to wrist-cutting."

Father Peter stepped into the corridor, slightly opened the first door to his left and peeked through the crack. On the other side was a diminutive flat, where two small, grey-eyed children, one boy and one girl, no older than two, sat on a grey, carpet floor. Father Peter stepped inside. Dirty laundry lay around in piles, and unwashed dishes covered the counter. One dish had fallen and broken into several pieces, and no effort had been made to clean the mess. The little boy toddled toward the kitchen. The girl began to cry.

"Eleanor, one of the littl'uns is cryin' again!" said a man's voice from another room.

A young girl, who looked about sixteen, with long, auburn hair, made her way over to the living room and picked up the girl.

"Now now, what's the matter, Darcy?" asked Eleanor.

Little Darcy pointed toward the kitchen. Her brother had made his way over to the broken dish on the floor, picked up a few pieces and was now examining them.

"Dalton, put that down, now!" said Eleanor, rushing toward Dalton.

He played with the pieces of ceramic and cut his wrist. He cried.

"This isn't the right memory," Isidora said to Father Peter, as she watched the scene unfold over his shoulder. "Let's go."

Father Peter and Isidora stepped out of the room and shut the door. They entered the room across the hall.

Inside, teenage Darcy sat on top of a bunk bed and Dalton lay in the bunk below her, reading a book. Across was another bunk bed, on top of which a girl with blonde hair spoke to Darcy. In the bottom bunk below her, another teen was fast asleep. Father Peter had seen enough foster homes in his life to recognize it as one.

"Have either of you ever tried cutting before?" asked the girl.

"No, and I shan't," said Darcy with a shudder.

Dalton's eyes lifted from his book and he listened in on the conversation.

"It's harmless. Even quite thrilling. And it takes the pain inside away."

"I'd rather have pain inside than cut me wrists," said Darcy.

"You should try. Just to see what it's like."

The blonde girl reached under her pillow and pulled out a kitchen knife. She leaned forward over her bed and handed it to Darcy. She looked at it, and looked back up at the girl, hesitantly. She gestured a wrist-cutting motion. Dalton jumped out of his bed.

"Don't even think about it. You'll go mad, like Mother."

The blonde girl laughed. "Your sister's already mad. She thinks she can tell the future."

"I can," said Darcy. "And I know you're going to die soon."

"I wish I were dead. I don't feel anything." The girl hopped out of her bed and left the room.

"How will she die?" asked Dalton.

"She's going to hang herself, and her neck will snap. And then she'll burn in Hell for all eternity."

"Do you ever have nice visions of the future?"

"Yes. You're going to get into all the best schools." Darcy smiled at her brother. He smiled back.

"Wrong memory," said Father Peter.

They exited the room and opened the next door.

Inside, Eleanor looked about ten years older than she had in the memory they'd last seen her in. Her grey eyes looked lifeless, and her undereye circles sank deep into her face, revealing the outline of her skull. Her emaciated, corpse-like figure sat on a torn-up sofa, and she stared blankly at a television. A preadolescent Dalton took a seat next to her. She ignored him.

"Mother, Darcy wants to watch football tonight, but I'm sick of football," he said. Eleanor didn't move. Dalton took her arm and tugged it. "Mother, I don't want to watch football."

Without moving, she acknowledged his request. "Mother doesn't either," she said. "Mother doesn't want to watch anything."

Dalton looked at the television, and back to Eleanor. "But you're watching the telly now," he said.

"Fuck off." She pushed Dalton off the sofa. "Why the fuck aren't you in school?"

"It's Saturday."

"Aren't you a clever boy. So much cleverer than your daft ol' ma."

Dalton frowned. Eleanor looked at him.

"Tell me, since you're so clever, I could use your advice." She patted the seat next to her and he came back.

"I would be happy to offer some insight," said Dalton.

Eleanor showed Dalton her forearm, took his finger, and placed it on her wrist.

"If I want to die, should I cut my wrist horizontally, like this, or vertically, like this?" She guided his finger in the two different directions.

Dalton cautiously pulled his hand away. "Transversely oriented deep wrist injuries can certainly cause a lot of damage, particularly to your nerves and tendons. Longitudinally oriented cuts will involve less injuries to nerves and tendons, but more damage to the radial artery, which is arguably more lethal," he stated, staring at the screen, avoiding the empty look in his mother's eyes.

A door opened and footsteps made their way down the hallway. The smell of beer filled the room. A middle-aged man walked in, holding onto the wall for balance. He held a half empty bottle in his hand. He broke the bottle against the wall, and pieces of glass fell as beer spilled on the grey carpeted floor. He threw the half of the bottle he still held in his hand onto the sofa, which landed between Eleanor and Dalton. A few more pieces of glass broke off the bottle. A sliver of the glass lodged itself in Dalton's wrist. He pulled it out, examined the blood-tipped shard and put it in the ashtray on the beer can-strewn coffee table.

"Go on then, Eleanor. Test his theory," said the man. He smiled, revealing several missing teeth.

Eleanor handed the bottle to Dalton and held out her arm. He held the broken bottle in his hands and stared at it.

"Go ahead, your ma wants to die," she said.

Dalton didn't move.

The man grabbed Eleanor by the wrist and dragged her into the kitchen, where he yelled at her and repeatedly shoved her into the wall.

"You wonder why that boy's so strange? Look at his ma. A bloody lunatic."

Eleanor didn't react, accepting her situation in indifferent resignation. Dalton ran out of the flat and joined Darcy, who was seated on the curb. Her dark hair was braided back. She held her hands together, connected at the fingertips, forming a circle around a spider. The spider climbed into the palm of her hand, and she cupped her hands together, trapping the creature. She turned around and smiled at Dalton, holding out her hands to him in an offering manner.

"No thank you," said Dalton.

"Father Peter," said Isidora, grabbing the priest's shoulder. "Wrong memory."

Father Peter followed Isidora out of the room. They stood in the dark corridor and headed for the next door. Isidora went inside. Father Peter hesitated for a moment, unsure how much more he could stand seeing. He entered.

Inside, Father Peter was overwhelmed with a desolate disconnect from reality. The world seemed to fade away, and sound was no more than a distant echo. He felt numb and apathetic. He wanted his miserable existence to end. He watched Dalton McGovern, sitting on the floor of his kitchen, force a knife into his forearm and drag it down to his wrist. He put the knife into his other hand, and manically cut at his other arm until he fell, laying in a pool of his own blood. He got back up and repeated these gestures.

The old man cackled. Father Peter reached for his toolbox, only to realize he no longer had it.

"Isidora," he called out. "Where are you?"

Isidora appeared to have vanished. Father Peter walked across the flat aimlessly, looking for anything that resembled a religious symbol to defend himself against the old man. He found nothing.

He tried turning the tap on, hoping he could bless the water, but nothing came out. There was a hissing behind him. Father Peter turned around and found himself face to face with the old man.

"Have you lost something?" asked the demon.

Father Peter felt something burn his shoulder. He looked over. Isidora was gripping him. Her eyes were completely black, except for the irises, which had turned from blue to yellow. Her lips were black, and her rotten skin was an ashy grey. She held up Father Peter's toolbox and grinned. It caught fire and burned away.

"Isidora, I know you're still in there, somewhere," said Father Peter. "You can still be saved."

Dalton, whom until that moment seemed unaware of his surroundings, spoke to Father Peter.

"It's useless, Father," he said. "You can't save anyone. I can't save anyone. It's all loneliness, desolation, and suffering. Just give up already. Your God did a long time ago."

Father Peter rushed over to Dalton and knelt by him.

"That's not the Dr. McGovern I know," said Father Peter, taking the knife away from him. "The Dr. McGovern I know always searches for a solution."

"And where did that get us? Look at them. Look at you. Look at me. We're all dead or dying, we're all part of someone else's sick game, and there's nothing any of us can do about it. We think we have control over our lives, that we have free will. And then something absurd occurs that throws all of our plans out the window, destroys our understanding of the world, and leaves us floating aimlessly in endless non-existence It's unbearable, Father."

Father Peter took one of Dalton's fingers and brought it to the opposite forearm.

"Dalton, since you're so clever, I could use your advice. Would you heal more efficiently like this, or like this?" He had Dalton trace his finger over his wounds, and they closed up. He took Dalton's other hand and did the same to his other arm.

"It would appear my advice is not required," Dalton replied.

Father Peter felt burning arms wrap around his body from behind. Isidora pressed up against him, rested her head on his shoulder and brought a hand to his face, running a finger against his lips. Father Peter stood still, resisting the urge to throw her off him, despite the blistering pain of her body and her touch.

"I know you love me," said Isidora with a laugh. "Join me, and it won't hurt anymore."

Father Peter looked into Isidora's eyes. As evil as they appeared, they had the expression of a drowning victim, desperately clinging to her life, even if it meant dunking those trying to save her.

"The two of you would do anything to avoid suffering, wouldn't you?" asked Father Peter. "Isidora, the minute things get tough, you have to latch onto whatever will allow you to escape how you're feeling."

Isidora pulled away from him and frowned. "You don't know anything about me nor what I've been through," she hissed.

"When you were alive, you drank. And now, here you are, accepting to be one of Satan's pawns to avoid suffering and fighting off his evil within you. Frankly, it's pathetic. Don't you have any willpower?"

Isidora glared and crossed her arms.

Father Peter turned to Dalton. "And you. You just shut down your feelings to avoid facing the bad ones. But the good ones make life worth living. If you shut down your feelings, you won't have any reason to live. And life doesn't end when you die. It goes on eternally, and one way or another, you will have to suffer. There is no end, only salvation."

Dalton rolled his eyes.

The old man stepped toward the group, towering over them. "Father Peter, when will you learn that people are sick and tired of being told how to behave by priests who can't even behave themselves?" said the old man. "They're sick of your hypocrisy. No one wants to suffer. Life is about avoiding suffering. Happiness is the temporary relief from suffering. Imagine if that release could be eternal. God's sick world is full of pain and misery. Why have salvation, when you can choose liberty?"

"Suffering is not fatal nor final," said Father Peter, standing up to face the old man. "Suffering produces perseverance. Perseverance, character. And character, hope."

Father Peter turned to Isidora and held out his hand to her, knowing it would burn him. She stayed seated, her arms crossed, and stared at his hand, avoiding his eyes.

"Isidora, when I first saw into your soul, I saw how fragile you were. There's no strength in repression; it's an escape. Accept that you have to endure hardship and you will build the strength of character you need for salvation."

"Easy to say," said Isidora, who made eye contact with Father Peter and quickly looked away. "It's easy to face who you are when you have a clean slate. When you've never done things that you regret. Not everyone is like you, Father, carefree and joyfully present-minded. Some of us have baggage. And living with what we have done is the worst torture of all. I'm not fragile, I'm damaged goods."

"Our sins can't be erased; they are a part of who we are, and who we become. But what you choose to do with those mistakes belongs to you. You can avoid facing them and save yourself the suffering that comes with self-loathing. Or, you can do your best to make up for your wrongdoings and the harm you've caused. If you can face your mistakes, you can find redemption. And you will be forgiven."

Isidora looked into his eyes and shook her head. "What happened to Stanley... nothing I can do can repair the damage I've caused. He will be scarred for life, and it's all my fault." The yellow in her eyes faded back into their natural pale blue colour.

"He's tougher than you think," said Father Peter with a smile. "He's resilient, and he'll overcome the suffering he's experienced. If he can, so can you. Trying times change people; there's nothing you can do to go back to the normal world you once took for granted. But what you choose to do with those changes belongs to you. Redemption is the key toward salvation."

Father Peter turned to Dalton, who sat on the ground, staring at his own reflection in his blood on the floor.

"Dalton, you have to persevere. You can't anticipate what life has in store for you. There isn't much you can actually control. You never have, and you never will. You have to face the present state in which you find yourself, and work with that reality."

Dalton looked up at Father Peter. "What am I supposed to do?

Accept that the world will fall apart, in bitter resignation?"

Father Peter shook his head. "Dream, take action, but accept that you can't calculate and manipulate the world around you. Embrace your fate. When you find the right path, God will light the way. You will find hope."

Dalton nodded hesitantly. "But I've ruined it. By trying to manipulate the world, I destroyed it. There's nothing more I can do."

"Take responsibility for your mistakes. Get out of your head and face the mess you've created. Fix it."

"Dalton, Isidora, ignore the silly priest," said the old man. "He knows we're going to win the war. And when we win, suffering will end, once and for all. The sick God of martyrdom and the veneration of pain will fall, and freedom shall prevail."

Dalton looked anxiously at Father Peter upon hearing of an imminent war and stood up abruptly. "The apocalypse," said Dalton. "My God, I've started the apocalypse."

"Yes, He's your God," said Father Peter. "And it's not too late to stop it all."

"First, we'll have to do something about that bloody old man in Dalton's head," said Isidora, standing up. Her skin was regaining its pink undertones.

"Pray with me," said Father Peter, holding Dalton's knife in his hand. The three walked toward the old man, who backed away.

"In the name of the Father, the Son and the Holy Ghost," said Father Peter, which Isidora and Dalton echoed.

The knife in Father Peter's hand blazed in a bright blue flame. Isidora and Dalton each grabbed one of the old man's arms and pushed him down. The old man knelt; his arms were stretched out as though he were being crucified. Father Peter stood over him and held up the knife.

"Unclean old man, you are forgiven." He stabbed the old man between the eyes. He vanished into a pile of ash.

"Where did he go?" asked Isidora.

"When a soul is destroyed, they float in the void for all eternity," said Father Peter.

"All right, everyone out of my head, now," ordered Dalton.

CHAPTER TWELVE

Isidora lay on the floor, feeling all the agony fade away into a sense of euphoric relief. She opened her eyes, sat up, looked at her arms and observed her perfect skin. She touched her soft face and ran her hands through her silky blonde hair. She turned to Quentin, who still sat in the corner with his eyes shut.

"How do I look?" she asked. She wondered if her appearance was as pure as how her soul felt.

Quentin kept muttering limericks to himself. "There once was a bloody ol' man, who latched onto me neck with his hand... That's not a proper rhyme, is it?"

Isidora got up and walked over to Dalton, Stanley, and Father Peter.

"I saved your soul!" said Father Peter, observing her radiance.

Isidora disregarded the priest's remark and beamed at her nephew. Stanley ran into Isidora's arms and burst into tears. Her ethereal beauty filled the room as she hugged him back.

"I'm sorry for the things I said during that last dinner at my place," she told him. "And I'm sorry I didn't go after you when you ran away."

"Is the old man gone?" asked Stanley.

"He's gone."

Dalton cleared his throat. "Stanley, I suppose I owe you an apology too. You know, for letting the old man into my head and almost killing you."

Stanley ran over to Dalton and kicked him in the shin. Dalton grabbed his leg and complained that it would likely leave a bruise.

"Sorry, I was just checkin' to see if it hurt, to make sure it was really you," said Stanley.

Dalton looked over. Darcy stood over Karl, who was desperately trying to crawl away from her.

"Karl, what's going on?" asked Dalton. "What happened to your leg?"

"Stop her, please!" Karl wheezed.

Darcy stomped on Karl's head, killing him. Dalton ran over and stared at Karl's crushed skull. His face still wore an expression of terror. Dalton's eyes filled with tears, and all the rage he'd internalized for years surfaced at once. He grabbed Darcy and pinned her against the wall.

"What is the matter with you?" he yelled frantically, and slammed her against the wall once more, her concussed head hitting the wall behind her. Losing consciousness, her dead weight dragged Dalton to the ground, as he attempted to catch her.

"Dalton, stop!" yelled Isidora. "She's possessed!"

Sitting on the floor, Dalton cradled his sister in his arms. Her closed lids suddenly flew wide open, revealing her yellow irises. They faded back to their usual grey, though they were oddly pale; lifeless. Dalton placed two fingers on her neck but couldn't find her pulse. His hands trembled and weakened, causing him to drop her head. He felt an urge to get away from her as though it would distance himself from what he'd done.

*   *   *

The Pope arrived at the University of Liverpool's campus in a cab emblazoned with an image of the Beatles with their mop tops. The Bishop of Rome looked up at the red moon and smiled, knowing it symbolized the dawn of the apocalypse. Looking ahead toward the university, he could sense enough paranormal activity to find his way to the laboratory. The Supreme Pontiff of the Universal Church had brought with him a large, golden staff with a crucifix on top. Stephen, who had been studying late, stopped in his tracks as the Vicar of Christ swung the glass door open.

"Hey, you're one of my followers," Stephen told the Successor of the Prince of the Apostles by way of introduction.

The Pope gave Stephen a wink. "Do you know where I can find the crazy guy? The mad scientist?"

Stephen's eyes lit up. "Dr. McGovern! He's not mad, he's brilliant! Follow me."

Following Stephen, the Pope strode down the hallway toward the lab. He sensed a repelling, haunted aura emanating from the east wing of the building. Stephen's breathing grew increasingly rapid and audible.

As they approached the laboratory door, the Pope stepped ahead of Stephen and placed his staff in front of the student, stopping him from opening the door. The Pope turned to Stephen and smiled.

"You smell that?" asked the Pope.

Stephen took a step away from the door of the laboratory. "It's like rotten eggs. Or sulphur. With another awful smell. It reminds me of when my sister burned her hair with her curling iron. And... something metallic. And sweet. I'm not sure what it is, but it's awful."

The Pope laughed. "That's the smell of Hell! Tell me, what do you hear?"

Stephen took another step back, closed his eyes and concentrated. He grimaced. "There's something awful. A screeching sound. Or a hissing. I can't quite make it out, but it almost sounds like some ancient language. I'm not a student of the humanities, I'm not very familiar with such tongues."

"Old Aramaic! The demons of Hell still use it. Listen closely; what else do you hear?"

With his eyes still closed, Stephen's face softened. "It's beautiful, and glorious. Like a folkloric Celtic ballad, with anthemic triumph."

The Pope nodded. "Excellent. The angels are preparing for war. Now tell me, what do you see?"

Stephen opened his eyes. His face dropped, and he fell to the ground, cowering. Around him was a green fog emanating from under the closed laboratory door. He looked more closely. Dozens of pairs of eyes watched him. Whimpering, he crawled away from the door back down the hallway and struggled to get up. Finally getting back on his feet, Stephen darted away. The Pope laughed.

He turned back toward the door and pushed on it, but it was sealed shut. Stupid demon tricks. He brought his fingers to his forehead, his heart, and to each shoulder, forming the sign of the cross, as though entering a church. *Once the war is over, everything will be a church,* he thought.

His Holiness bent his head and prayed. "Though I walk through the valley of the shadow of death, I will fear no evil: for thou art with me; thy rod and thy staff they comfort me." He lifted his head and pried the door open with his staff.

When the Pope entered the laboratory, he looked around and grinned. At the far end of the laboratory, Dalton knelt by Darcy's dead body, next to Karl's and Edward's crushed heads. Over in the far-right corner lay Dr. Whalen's corpse and severed brain. In the far-left corner, half-demonic Quentin muttered to himself. To the right of the laboratory's centre lay Chief Constable Evelyn Glasgow's body. The Pope nodded in approval, assessing that she would make a good warrior. Immediately to his right, Father Peter, Isidora and Stanley stood along the wall. Immediately to his left was a great big void of eternal non-existence.

The Pope laughed. "I see we are having lots of fun!"

"Your Holiness!" said Father Peter, who rushed over and kissed his ring. "What a blessing it is to find you here. I could hug you."

The Pope waved him away in mild disgust and walked over to the Chief Constable's corpse.

"Where are my soldiers?" he asked and raised his hands heavenward. From their lifeless bodies, Darcy, Dr. Whalen and Chief Constable Glasgow's glowing souls stood up, awaiting command. Father Peter and Isidora stepped forward. The Pope nodded approvingly.

"Lots of beautiful women! Father Peter, this is the dream!" said the Pope. "Now, demons, I can feel your presence. Don't be little bitches, show yourselves."

The Pope raised his hands up once more. The entity which had possessed Dr. Whalen, Chief Constable Glasgow and Darcy appeared, her yellow eyes shining in the dark laboratory and her long, matted grey hair blending with the stone-like appearance of her skin. From the shadows, multiple red, black, yellow and white eyes peeked about, refusing to show themselves fully. Karl and Edward emerged from their corpses, their skin red and freshly burned. Karl's eyes were crimson, and Edward's white. The Pope laughed.

"*Vous êtes donc ben laittes esti,*" said the Pope. "Ugly demons all going to disappear in the void!"

The Pope ran his staff through the yellow-eyed entity. She screeched and fell to the floor. The other demons in the laboratory hissed. The Pope turned the staff downward and stabbed the yellow-eyed entity in the head with its crucifix-shaped tip. Her blood visibly boiled beneath her skin and the popping bubbles sounded like popcorn in the microwave. Her body burst, vanishing into a pile of ash that smelled of sulphur The Pope looked around expectantly, but the demons did nothing. He shrugged and walked over to Stanley and Dalton.

"And you two? Which side you choose?" It was unclear whether the Pope asked a question or gave an order.

"We're... alive," explained Dalton. "We like it that way."

The Pope grunted and went over to look at Quentin. His scaly appearance wasn't quite that of a demon, but was nonetheless ghastly.

"*Quessé ça, criss!* What the hell is the weird guy?" asked the Pope. Quentin opened his eyes, which lit up upon seeing the Pope.

"You're the Pope who, many years ago, tried to get elected to the Canadian Parliament," Quentin said. "I looked up the results when I heard about it. You were the Bloc Québécois candidate in the riding of Saint-Maurice. You lost by a bloody lot to the Liberal incumbent."

The Pope frowned. "What the fuck is wrong with you? You are like these mentally fucked people who remember weird shit for nothing?"

"It's a fun fact. It keeps me mind off this whole demon-transition thing," said Quentin.

"Fun facts are for faggots," said the Pope.

"That's homophobic," Karl's flaming soul hissed.

"But seriously. What the fuck is wrong with you? What is wrong with that face?" the Pope asked Quentin. A few more flakes fell from Quentin's forehead and sizzled on the floor.

"If you don't mind, I'm trying to concentrate on not becoming a bloody demon," said Quentin. "I will stay exactly who I want to be. A computer program who can do whatever the bloody hell he likes."

"*Tabarnak!*" said the Pope, slamming his staff against the floor. "You cannot do this shit. You have to move on to your afterlife state or we cannot start the war!"

"I don't give a bloody fuck about your war." Quentin shut his eyes. He felt that acknowledging his demonic state made the process accelerate.

"What if I do some Pope shit to make you one of my soldiers instead?" The Pope offered. He could do no such thing but wanted Quentin to give up on remaining a virtual being.

"Not interested."

The Pope stabbed in frustration at a few demons in the shadows, who vanished into ash.

Though he was now a demon, Karl hadn't lost his French. "*Pardonnez-moi, mais vous venez de commettre de nombreux crimes de guerre.* You can't just go around killing us for nothing," he said to the Pope. "Satan has informed us that the war has not started yet and that regardless, you, the Pope, do not have the authority to start the war. And you should know, we greatly outnumber you. Keep acting this way and we will legitimately be allowed to act in self-defence. Destroying souls is only legal during a divine war under the terms of article 23.6 of the Heavenly Realms Treaty of 1624."

Out of thin air, Karl pulled out an aged parchment scroll which appeared to be the original copy of the Treaty, and pointed to the article in question, showing it around the room. The scroll vanished, and a thick, brown, dusty book appeared in his hands, with *The Criminal Code of the Heavens* written in blood red. He flipped it open and pointed to page 1136.

"Destroying souls is an indictable offence punishable by up to three millennia in the pits of Hell. Right here, article 634.12 of *The Criminal Code of the Heavens*, everyone." Karl showed the page to the room. The book vanished once he felt he had sufficiently made his point to most of the souls present.

"Hang on. If the Pope doesn't have the authority to declare a war, then who does?" asked Isidora.

"Article 1364 of *The Civil Code of the Heavens* clearly states that only God's Paladin has the authority to declare a divine war," said Karl, now holding a thick, red book in his hands with golden letters.

"And who is God's Paladin?" asked Dalton.

"No one important," said the Pope. "Some ancient mythical bullshit."

"Article 7 of the *Interpretations Act of the Heavens* states that God's Paladin is the rightful successor of Saint Peter," said Karl, holding a dark blue book titled *Statutes of the Heavens*, written in silver.

"Saint Peter was the first Pope," said Darcy. "Therefore, the Pope *is* God's Paladin and he *does* have the authority to declare war. Go on, Your Holiness. Do it! We want a war!" She raised her fist in the air. Cheers followed.

"Wrong. Article 7.1 of the *Interpretations Act of the Heavens* defines the rightful successor of Saint Peter as his hereditary heir," said Karl.

"This is bullshit," said the Pope. "I've heard enough. I declare war!"

"That statement is invalid," said Karl.

"Saint Peter..." muttered Isidora. She turned to Father Peter. "What if you're God's Paladin? I mean, your name *is* Peter."

"Shut up!" said the Pope.

"Absolutely not," said Karl. "It would be a huge abuse of power on God's part for the Paladin, capable of declaring war among the Heavens, to be an exorcist, or should I say, a serial demon killer."

Father Peter smiled. He liked the idea of being a serial demon killer.

"Article 7.1.1 says God's Paladin is the only soul capable of being both a demon and a soldier of God."

"Wait, what the fuck, that's not right," said the Pope. "The annoying blonde is right. Father Peter is God's Paladin. The Church has been following the lineage of Saint Peter for centuries. He is the descendent of Saint Peter. That's why we sent him away to become an exorcist, like every other one of God's Paladins before him. To protect the democracy of the Vatican! We can't have hereditary heirs. It would compromise the legitimacy of the institution."

"Am I really that threatening to you?" said Father Peter with a grin.

"God's Paladin is Isidora," said Karl. "She's the only one who can choose to be either a demon or a soldier of God. Her will is our command."

Quentin laughed. "That sounds like Izzy. A real Goddess."

Isidora winked at him.

All eyes were on Isidora. The demons and the soldiers of God began to chant, *We want a war! We want a war!* Father Peter took Isidora's hand and shook his head.

"Don't do this, Isidora. You're not ready. You're still vulnerable."

Isidora pulled her hand away. "Stop trying to put me down just because you can sense that I am greater than you."

She stepped into the middle of the room, surrounded by chanting demons and angels. The Pope gave her a nod. She smiled and shrugged.

"Fine, I declare war."

The demons and soldiers cheered. The Pope knocked over countless demons with his staff and Darcy, wielding the chair she'd crushed Edward's head with, took on five demons at a time on her own. Karl stood up on a chair.

"Everyone, please settle down. This is all still very much illegal."

No one listened to Karl. Father Peter and Edward boxed, and Stanley watched, cheering and heckling. Isidora did her best to watch all of the combatants, assuming she had some kind of role arbitrating the war.

"Please, stop this at once!" Karl insisted. "According to article 1368 of *The Civil Code of the Heavens*, the apocalypse can only come into effect when the unnatural, the natural and the supernatural become one. Only then can God's Paladin make a declaration of war. Since Quentin is still part virtual, the unnatural world remains somewhat intact. Why do you think the Rapture hasn't occurred yet? Where is Jesus' epic return to Earth? Why would the entire apocalyptic battle be limited to this laboratory? This is not the apocalypse—this is a rumble!"

"Reason is pointless," said Dalton, who stood back, leaning against the wall, his arms crossed. "If they want to fight, let them fight. The whole thing is a bloody disaster."

Karl jumped down from the chair and flew over to Dalton.

"I'd kill you, but I can't tell if you're good or bad, and I don't want to accidentally give the other team another player," Karl said, joining Dalton against the wall.

"I just can't believe any of it," said Dalton. "It's bloody ridiculous."

"What can't you believe?" asked Karl. He reached for Dalton's hand and inadvertently burned him.

"That right there. It's ridiculous," said Dalton, showing Karl the burn mark on his hand. "It's ridiculous that you're a demon."

"I agree," said Karl. "I'm a kind person. I mean, I've committed some crimes, I may have enabled street gangs and terrorist organizations in carrying out attacks across Europe, but generally, I am nice. I always hold the door open for people and say please and thank you."

"You're not that kind," said Dalton. "You abandoned me when I was at my worst. I needed you to help me feel something again."

Karl shook his head. "You can't just go along expecting everyone else to solve your problems. We all have—or had—lives of own. Problems of our own. You need to take some responsibility and actively work toward helping yourself."

Dalton looked into Karl's evil eyes. "Just admit it. You're selfish. That's why you're a demon now."

"I'm selfish? *I'm* selfish? You're the one who thinks he's so much better than all of us peasants. You think the world revolves around you, and we do everything we can to satisfy you, but it's never enough. You expect everyone to be at your service. I moved to

Liverpool for you! Fucking Liverpool! And you still don't see how much we all sacrifice for you. The minute anyone criticizes you, you play the misunderstood genius card. You can't stand being questioned. You push everyone away and then you wonder why you're alone. You want to know why you're alone? Because you're unpleasant. Maybe I should kill you. You would probably be the worst demon of all. You would be an uber-demon who would kill everyone, and again, you would find yourself alone. And you would still manage to feel sorry for yourself and blame everyone else for your misery."

"It's ridiculous. I don't believe any of it. This isn't happening."

"Sure, deny everything. That will get you far."

"I'm serious, Karl. It doesn't make any sense. It's absurd. My mind is playing tricks on me. My perspective of things cannot possibly be accurate. No proper scientist would accept that what they see is what they get. There has to be some sort of explanation for all this madness. It is intellectually lazy to simply accept what appears to be the obvious truth."

"You have to accept that reality is much bigger than what you thought it to be."

Dalton smiled. "That's it! I must have missed something. I didn't fully consider the implications of my afterlife malfunctioning and what the consequences could be."

"Exactly. These are the consequences."

"These are how the consequences appear to us. But surely there is a scientific explanation behind the nature of these consequences." Dalton adjusted his shirt collar. "Now if you don't mind, I have a problem to solve."

*   *   *

Father Peter felt Edward had an unfair advantage in their boxing match. Every time he hit Edward, it burned him. He did his best, but by the end of the last round, he had a feeling he'd lost. Stanley walked up in between them and took their wrists.

"Ouch!" Stanley said, pulling his hand away from Edward's scorching skin. He frowned and raised Father Peter's arm in the air.

"Winner!" he declared.

"Rubbish," said Edward. "You only gave Father Peter the win because it hurt to touch me."

Stanley and Edward argued over the outcome of the match and Father Peter ambled over to Isidora, who was explaining to a handful of demons why Darcy and the Chief Constable were not unfair advantages for God's side due to their military and police backgrounds, respectively.

"There are way more of you than there are of God's soldiers. I think Darcy and the Chief Constable are great equalizers in that respect."

The demons grunted and went back to fighting Darcy and Chief Constable Glasgow. The demons clawed and bit at them. They, in turn, hit the demons with chairs, laptops, binders, notebooks, and anything they could find in the laboratory. Behind them, Dr. Whalen—who had strapped a demon to a table and sawed open its brain—was now testing where the demon was most vulnerable by poking its brain arbitrarily. Gnashing its razor-sharp teeth, the demon howled and swore, kicked and struggled against her. A few demons shot blazing balls of fire to get to Dr. Whalen, but the Pope bludgeoned them with his staff.

"Isidora," said Father Peter, approaching her. "I'm sorry if I offended you somehow."

Isidora crossed her arms and turned away from him. "That's the worst apology," she said. "I'm not offended. You were patronizing, and I didn't like it. When we were inside Dalton's mind, you made me feel like I needed you, like I depended on you. In reality, I was the one who was able to understand Dalton's mind, I was the one who successfully tracked down the old man, and I had a special ability to switch from demon to soldier of God all along. I thought I needed you to save me. I saved myself, and you tried to take credit for it."

Father Peter reached toward her, gently took her shoulders and turned her around to face him. "I was just trying to help... you seemed to be struggling with the whole demon thing." He brought his hands down and reached for her hand, but she took a step back and crossed her arms once more.

"You're an exorcist, and you're good at killing demons, I'll give you that. But don't pretend you know me, like you have me all figured out. You've acted that way since the day we met and it's infuriating. You have no idea what you're talking about. And you had the nerve to tell me how to improve myself, when all along, I was exactly who I should be. God's Paladin."

"I know my arrogance sometimes gets the best of me. I'm sorry. I would love to get to know you better." He stepped forward, held her hands and smiled. "You're the smartest woman I've ever met, and I'm so happy to have you in my life. I spend the greatest time with you."

Isidora pulled her hands away. "I don't exist for your entertainment. Now run along," she said with a dismissive wave. "There are plenty of demons to deal with."

Isidora decided to take a break from arbitrating the battle and sat down next to Quentin. He was still leaning with his back against the wall. His arms were wrapped around his bent knees.

"Are you aware you are single-handedly preventing the apocalypse from occurring with your stubbornness?" asked Isidora with a half-smile.

"I don't give a fuck about any of that. I'm not turnin' into a bloody demon."

Edward sped past the two of them, fleeing from Darcy. She seemed to have figured out how to generate a divine electrical current from her hands and could now shock demons at will. She shot two blue bolts at Edward. He fell to the floor and moaned. From across the room, Dr. Whalen suggested that Darcy should aim for the neocortex next time for better results.

Isidora smiled at Quentin. "I think not turning into a demon is a wise choice. Darcy appears to have developed quite the demon-slaying abilities."

Stanley limped over and sat on the other side of Quentin.

"Eddie's a sore loser. He can't stand that Father Peter is harder than him," Stanley griped.

Isidora and Stanley each reached for one of Quentin's hands. They were hot, as though he had a bad fever. He let go of his knees and stretched out his legs, letting his arms fall on either side of him, holding Stanley and Isidora's hands back, which he found oddly small.

"Tell me more about how Eddie can't fight," Quentin said.

*   *   *

Father Peter wasn't awfully familiar with anger. He was generally content. He rarely failed to get what he wanted; life always seemed to treat him well. He assumed it was God's reward for his stalwart faith. He always believed there was something special about himself. He'd occasionally overhear whispers among Church officials when he passed by them in the halls of the Vatican. There seemed to be a sort of great secret around him, but without trying to understand it, he assumed it was simply that he was wonderful and that the others recognized his specialness. Someone had to be God's favourite. He was proud it was him.

Upon learning they had all mistaken him for God's Paladin, a world Father Peter never fully understood came crashing down. The subtle, pervasive admiration he received was all based on a false assumption. Sure, he was an excellent exorcist. Now it struck him that he probably had been heaped with excessive praise for his accomplishments, with the church's elite presuming he was the divine heir of a lineage destined to rule the church and ultimately start the apocalypse. Was he even as competent as he thought he was? Were his powers special in any way, or did his resolute faith allow him to be nothing more than another channel for God's glory?

Seeing Darcy blasting demons into oblivion with electric bolts shooting from her palms, he understood that not only was he not the greatest exorcist in the world, he might not even be the greatest exorcist in the room. It was dispiriting to discover that he could spend his whole life training to be an exorcist and that Darcy —a newbie at demon skirmishing—had such miraculous abilities. Her commitment to the church throughout her life extended little beyond wearing a necklace with a little golden cross, eating chocolate for Easter and getting drunk on Christmas.

Father Peter didn't even feel like trying to serve God anymore and almost wished to give up and let the nasty little demons do their worst. At least he wouldn't have to think about how God's *actual* Paladin had no interest in sleeping with him. Father Peter's hands clenched into fists of rage seeing Isidora sitting with Quentin and Stanley like they were one big family.

He strode over to the Pope and attempted to yank the staff out of his hands.

"What the fuck is wrong with you? *Décaliss*," said the Pope. He pushed Father Peter away.

"I want to kill some demons. Give me the staff," he said, and grabbed it by the middle. The stronger of the two, the Pope wrenched it back to himself again.

"This is my staff. After all those years of training, when finally you are in a real battle, the only thing you can think to do is steal an old man's staff? That's it, after all the money the church has invested in you?" said the Pope.

"You're a fraud, a politician, and you don't deserve the staff any more than me." Father Peter tugged at the staff but the Pope had a firm grip.

"I was legitimately elected Pope. Fuck monarchies. Fuck the Queen of England and fuck God's Paladin. I'm the Leader of the Church. I get the staff."

"You're such a hypocrite. Vatican City is an absolute elective monarchy."

"Not under my watch. Now release my staff, you useless son of a bitch."

"No. I want it. Because you wrongly believed that I was God's Paladin, I didn't get to live my own life, and was sent away to be an exorcist. You took enough from me. You could at least give me the staff."

The Pope burst into laughter. "I was just thinking of this. I was wondering how the hell we fucked up figuring out who is God's Paladin. Then I thought about it and saw where we got confused. We were pretty close. Your father was just like you: a travelling exorcist and a smug, horny bastard. At some point he got some woman he met once in a UK pub pregnant. We didn't think the bastard child could be the heir of Saint Peter, so we ignored this little girl and focused on you because anyways, special abilities were developing in you already. I mean, I call you a bastard, because you're *un criss de cave*, but she is actual bastard. You understand what I am saying? Isidora is your half-sister. You want to fuck your sister!"

"You sick, lying old pontiff."

The Pope laughed so hard he could hardly breathe. "I'm sorry, but it is so obvious. You look so much the same! Why do you think you are so drawn to her? Because you are in love with yourself."

"Give me the staff."

"Over my dead body."

"If you insist." Father Peter sucker-punched him and plucked the staff from the Holy Father's unconscious hands.

Father Peter began chasing after demons, plunging the staff into their brains, each one he destroyed reduced to a puff of acidic demon dust. He was so overcome by maniacal fury he entered an almost dream-like state, in which he was completely unaware of his actions. The demons started to gang up on him, corralling him from three sides and forcing him ever nearer to the eternal void in the laboratory. The closer he got to the void, the more ash hung in the air from combusted demons, blurring his surroundings. He gasped for breath and struggled to keep his stinging eyes open. He felt something acidic, razor-sharp and wet sink into his neck and realized a demon's jaw was locked onto him from behind. It sank its teeth further and gnawed at his spine. He tried to push it off, but a burning in his chest, his face, and his stomach paralyzed him in agony. He screamed as his skin began to fry. His hands weakened, and something jerked the staff away from him as he became overwhelmed by a burning sensation covering his entire body. Still in a haze, an oppressive force surrounded him, restrained him, and was killing him. Demons piled up on him, and he could no longer see anything but sharp, jagged nails, evil, empty eyes and rotten mouths and teeth. But the sound of demonic shrieks of terror pierced his ears and snapped him back to reality. He felt a great weight lift off of him as the demons on top of him turned into ash.

The golden staff illuminated the room around him. Father Peter watched as Pope Clement XV wielded it, killing the dozens of demons who had ganged up on him. They burst into piles of ash as the Pope jumped around whacking them, looking more like a ninja than an old man. He twirled his staff, teasing the demons before swatting them into the void like pesky flies. After the demons were gone, the Pope looked at Father Peter and laughed.

"*Voyons donc*, Father Peter. Storming a bunch of demons, your strength fuelled by the Seven Deadly Sins. What did you expect would happen?" The Pope was visibly tired, leaning against his staff to catch his breath. Still, he laughed.

"I'm sorry I hit you." Father Peter wiped some of the ash off himself but couldn't get up from the ground due to the agonizing burns across his body.

"Don't worry. You hit like a little girl." The staff wobbled and the Pope nearly lost his balance. He laughed it off.

"Thank you for saving me." Father Peter's voice was hoarse and faint.

The Pope looked the priest up and down and he shook his head.

"You look like shit. Go make yourself useful while you still can."

Father Peter tried to pick himself up off the floor, but the pain was too great. He was beginning to see nothing but the void.

"Peter Nightingale, you must get up." Hearing his full name pronounced aloud was oddly grounding for Father Peter.

"I can't. What's the point, anyway? My existence is pointless."

"Don't be a smug bastard. You don't know why God put you here. Tell me, Peter. What are you?"

Father Peter paused. "An exorcist."

"And what does an exorcist do?"

Father Peter propped himself up on his elbows and leaned back on his forearms. He looked the Pope in the eye. "He kills demons."

"Then you know what to do."

A shadowy figure rose up from the ashes behind the Pope. It was Edward. Before Father Peter could say anything to alert the Pope, Edward grabbed the Pope from behind and clawed at his neck and face, poisoning his bloodstream with acidic green venom.

The Pope backed up, winked at Father Peter, and threw himself into the void, dragging along Edward, destroying them both. He left behind nothing but his staff. Father Peter reached for it and raised himself to his feet.

Transcending the burning pain of his body, the heartbreak from Isidora's rejection, the grief of losing the Pope, Father Peter focused on one thing only: he was an exorcist, a soldier of God, and he would kill demons. With the power of his mighty faith, he plunged the staff into countless demons, and nothing could get in his away, except his soul, which, with each stroke of the staff, was slipping away into the void.

CHAPTER THIRTEEN

Dalton tried to turn on his computer, without any luck. He nonetheless tapped repeatedly on his keyboard, expecting something to happen.

"Didn't Einstein say the definition of insanity is doing the same thing over and over again and expecting different results?" asked Darcy, who took a seat next to him with a smile.

"I'm so sorry I killed you," said Dalton. "I had no idea—"

"It's all right," she said, braiding her hair. "Now let's find a way out of this mess. Why won't your computer start?"

"Nothing seems to get it started again. The servers are all blown up. It's hopeless."

"And yet, Quentin still seems to have a link to your program."

"I know."

"Then surely there's some way of getting it running again. Let's retrace our steps. How did it break?"

"I got hacked... by God, apparently... and everything stopped working, and then that replaced the screen." Dalton pointed toward the void.

"If God broke it, God can fix it. It just needs a little power."

Darcy showed Dalton the electric energy running through her hands. She aimed two bolts at the dead servers. In a matter of seconds, they began running again. Dalton's personal computer screen lit up, but the void remained present.

"Now what?" asked Darcy.

Dalton typed a series of numbers and letters that Darcy didn't even try to understand. "I need to figure out what the nature of that void is," said Dalton. "The void is the source of the malware that broke my system. If I can understand it, I can beat it."

Darcy nodded hesitantly, looking into the abyss. The realm of emptiness was oddly compelling, almost hypnotic, drawing all her attention to it. It seemed to be slowly spinning around itself, affected by some kind of gravitational force. "I think there's a little more to it than your ordinary malware, love."

Dalton shook his head and kept typing, furiously. "I need to figure out what it is. I can't just keep brushing it off as eternal uncertainty and avoiding having to face it. Everything we take for granted was at one time uncertain, until it was understood."

As he typed, Darcy blasted any demons who tried to approach them. Several times, Dalton brought his hands up to his head, muttered, *no, no, no, fuck,* slammed his keyboard with his fists, got out of his chair, circled around it, and sat back down.

"Persevere," said Father Peter, approaching the two of them from behind, clutching the Pope's staff. "You'll find hope."

Darcy turned and jumped up from her chair upon seeing Father Peter. He was covered in burn marks and was drenched in green acid.

"What happened to you?" she asked.

"Killed some demons with what little strength I had left."

"How did you find any?" asked Dalton, looking at his computer helplessly. "The strength to keep going?"

Father Peter remembered the desolate feeling, the disconnection from reality, that overcame him inside Dalton's mind and realized how similar he'd felt when he blindly stormed the demons in anger. He recalled how the Pope's staff illuminated the room when he'd saved him, not from the demons, but his own mindset.

"Dr. McGovern, I know how lost you are. And nothing a priest like me or a psychic like your sister could say would ever bring you comfort or help you understand life's meaning. Your mistake was giving up on trying to understand the world, opting to create your own instead. Others have made the mistake of failing to understand how you see the world and trying to impose their own understanding of it onto you as if that would free you of your angst. How did I find the strength to kill those demons with the little life inside me I had left? I remembered who I was: an exorcist. And you, Dr. McGovern, are a scientist. You will find life's meaning, if you keep trying, in your own way. Tell me, Dr. McGovern: how does a scientist give meaning to his environment?"

Dalton smiled. "As Lavoisier said, 'we must trust to nothing but facts: These are presented to us by Nature, and cannot deceive. We ought, in every instance, to submit our reasoning to the test of experiment, and never to search for truth but by the natural road of experiment and observation.' Words to live by, even though he was later guillotined."

Father Peter fell to his knees, dropping the staff. Darcy raced over to him and held him.

"Don't worry love, nothing a little holy water can't fix," she said.

"Alas, there is no holy water in this laboratory," Father Peter said with a laugh, which turned into a coughing fit.

"Now, now, get some rest; you'll recover soon enough."

Father Peter shook his head. "You know just as well as I do that there is no hope for me. I can feel myself fading into the void."

Darcy held his hand as he rested his head against her shoulder.

"Picture something in your mind you really like," said Darcy, stroking his hair. "Something that makes you smile."

"I don't need to," said Father Peter, as he admired Darcy's perky breasts. "What I see is perfect."

Dalton felt something soft brush up his leg. He looked down. It was Clyde.

"Perhaps your friend could be of some assistance," Father Peter said to Dalton. "Isidora had a theory you'd done something to the rats to have greater control over their codes in the virtual reality."

"Of course!" said Dalton. He grabbed Clyde, took a pen from his desk, and opened a stitch on the side of the rat's body. He carefully used the tip of the pen to fish out a chip from under its skin. Clyde nipped at Dalton to get away. Dalton let him go once he'd removed the chip. It was approximately the size of the tip of a needle. He brought it over to Father Peter.

"Here, find a way to consume this," Dalton told Father Peter. "By having you bring this chip along with you to your journey into desolation, I should be able to retrieve data on the void and hack it back."

Father Peter reached into his pocket and pulled out a small bag full of cocaine. He poured the content of the bag onto the floor next to him and Dalton placed the chip into the mix. Father Peter rolled out of Darcy's arms and onto the floor, blocked one nostril with his hand and snorted all the cocaine as well as the chip.

"That should work," said Dalton.

The priest winked at Dalton. "Remember, my dude: nothing is lost, nothing is created, everything is transformed."

Father Peter vanished into a pile of cocaine.

*   *   *

Quentin Campbell gripped Stanley and Isidora's hands and pictured all the things in the world that he liked. Maps. Beer. Boxing. Visual representations of data. Football. Sex. Sex in a fire. Fire. Hellfire. Eternal damnation.

"Quentin!" said Isidora, nudging him gently. "Focus. Your skin is peeling faster."

"It's getting harder," said Quentin. "I don't know how much longer I can go on like this."

Stanley flicked open his switchblade and brought it to Quentin's neck. "Don't you dare go soft on me."

Quentin smiled at Stanley. It hurt to pull his cheeks back. He could feel his skin crack with every movement he made. But in that moment, he felt like a proud parent.

"Good lad." Quentin patted Stanley on the back. It burned the child a little, but Stanley knew he had to be hard and not make a fuss or he would lose all credibility.

The three watched Chief Constable Glasgow and Dr. Whalen take on a dozen demons together. They were a surprisingly effective team. The Chief Constable was a good fighter, and Dr. Whalen would finish them off with her surgical tools once they lay helplessly on the floor. However, they were terribly outnumbered, and it was difficult to say for how much longer they could hold off so many evil entities.

"We're running out of time," said Quentin. "If I become a demon, the apocalypse will start and there won't even be any soldiers of God left in the laboratory to hold back the gates of Hell over there." He pointed to the void.

"I thought you didn't care about any of that," said Isidora.

Quentin looked at Stanley and Isidora. "I might care a little."

The demons split up Dr. Whalen and the Chief Constable. Though the Chief Constable managed to fight off her group, six demons piled up on Dr. Whalen, scratching her, taking out her eyes; biting her, chewing off her nose; spewing acid on her, tearing off her limbs, poking her with her own tools, smothering her.

"Fanny, hang on!" said the Chief Constable to Dr. Whalen as she struggled against a demon, shielding herself from its jaw and claws with the back of a chair.

"It's too late for me, Evelyn. Remember to aim for the neocortex." Dr. Whalen vanished into a pile of luminous angel dust.

Watching the scene unfold, Stanley gasped and Quentin's head dropped. "Two left," murmured Quentin. "Two soldiers of God, and an endless number of demons."

"The two best," said Isidora, squeezing his hand. "Darcy and the Chief Constable can hold them back. Just focus on yourself."

"That's right," said Dalton from the desk of his computer. "I will need you soon, Mr. Campbell, so don't you dare turn into a demon."

*   *   *

Dalton watched reams of data appear on the screen of his computer. He shook his head from side to side in small, rapid movements, and it was unclear whether he was gesturing the word "no" or whether this motion enabled him to read faster.

"It's chaotic," Dalton said to Darcy. "I can't figure out what this section here means." He pointed to some code on the screen.

"It looks all the same to me," said Darcy.

"Darcy, I could use a hand over here," said Chief Constable Glasgow.

"Perhaps you would be most useful assisting her," Dalton suggested.

Darcy stood up and shot several bolts of divine electricity through the demons between her and the Chief Constable. Dalton ignored their battle and focused on his own, his eyes locked on the screen.

I can tell this is the point where the priest entered the void due to the absence of external stimulation, thought Dalton. *But temporally, geographically, it's nonsensical. It's like he's everywhere at all times, and nowhere ever. What the bloody hell am I supposed to do with this kind of information?*

Someone pulled out the chair next to Dalton. Karl sat down and angled the chair toward the screen.

"I never understood what you found so fascinating about series of numbers and letters on a screen."

Dalton frowned. "I never understood what you found so fascinating about poorly worded laws in terribly organized books."

"I didn't. I did it for the money."

"I know."

"I did a lot of things for money."

"I know."

"I left you because you weren't earning as much money as I'd hoped."

Dalton turned away from his computer screen and looked at Karl. "You can't be serious."

"I thought, computers are the future, law is a dying profession, he's clever, he'll design some sort of app and make us both millionaires. Instead, look at what you chose to do with your talent. You ended the world. Well done!" Karl sarcastically applauded.

"I'm trying to focus on fixing that. If you don't mind, please go back to whatever it is you demons do in your spare time." Dalton turned back toward the screen.

Karl kept his eyes glued on Dalton. "Give up already. Science can't solve everything. Some things are simply too much for the human mind to handle."

"Not mine."

Karl moved in closer to Dalton and stroked his arm. He realized he burned him upon seeing the marks he'd left on his skin. Dalton, wholly absorbed in the task at hand, did not so much as flinch.

"Tell me, how can you possibly be so close-minded as to turn a blind eye to the divine phenomenon happening right behind you?" inquired Karl. "It's a miracle, Dalton. Stop trying to make sense of it in scientific terms. It's pointless."

"What a stupid thing to say. I can't believe I ever dated you."

"Just give up, Dalton. You hate the world. The only reason you can't stand seeing it fall apart is because you're not the one controlling its downfall. Accept that you're useless. You've always been useless, and you always will be. You had it right when you tried to kill yourself."

"Shut it."

Karl sneered. "You really are no more than a burden. You were a burden to your mother until you drove her mad; you were a burden on me until you drove me away; and you were a burden to Darcy until you killed her. You are an unbearable human being, and the reason you cannot stand being alive is because you experience the world through that miserable little mind of yours."

"Seriously, Karl. Shut it."

Karl edged in closer and whispered in Dalton's ear. "The only reason you haven't tried to kill yourself again yet is because of your vanity. You think you're doing the world a service by staying alive. You hope one day you will be recognized for your imaginary greatness. But you won't ever be. You aren't great. You aren't as clever as you think you are. You are a useless, dependent, selfish waste of oxygen. Kill yourself, Dalton. Cut your wrists and do it right this time, you incompetent, pathetic fool. Open up that artery and make sure you die. Do it!" Karl's evil eyes widened, and he broke out into an unnaturally broad grin.

Dalton kept his eyes fixed on the screen, resisting the urge to acknowledge Karl. "I have a theory about the nature of the void."

"Of course, you do, you twisted little narcissist."

"If two protons collide, they can create a minuscule black hole."

"You say that like I would care."

"The collision would create a small opening of interdimensional space where the laws of physics aren't the same as the ones we have here on Earth."

Karl's grin dropped and his eyes lacked any expression.

"You see, in string theory, there are ten different dimensions. Dimensions five through ten include all possible futures and past events, even in realities that don't abide by the laws of physics as we know them."

Karl frowned.

"Ordinarily, if such interdimensional space had enough gravity to interact with our world, it would grow at the speed of light and destroy everything as we know it, ending our world's existence and changing the laws of physics of our universe. However, somehow, my program seems to have frozen this interdimensional bubble, allowing passage through different dimensions by travelling in what we've been referring to as 'the void.'"

Karl considered sinking his nails into Dalton's neck and ripping open his jugular.

"The void isn't a void at all, you see. It's an interdimensional portal."

Karl thought it might be easier to just grab him by the head and snap his neck.

"How would you like to test my theory?"

"I beg your pardon?" asked Karl.

Dalton turned around and nodded at Darcy. She blasted Karl with her electric bolts, sending him into the void, and went back to fighting demons with the Chief Constable.

"Quentin, could you please come over here?" asked Dalton. Isidora and Stanley helped Quentin up and seated him next to Dalton.

"I appear to have inadvertently created an interdimensional portal."

"I hate it when that happens," replied Quentin. He picked up the pen Dalton had used on Clyde and began drawing a black hole on the desk.

"At the moment, it is nearly frozen, enabling relatively safe passage for virtual entities, not unlike what you experienced crossing over from my virtual world. However, I fear it is slowly expanding. The more it expands, the more it changes the laws of physics of our universe, which explains all this chaos. Should you lose touch with your virtual self, I fear the portal will expand at the speed of light, becoming a Cosmic Death Bubble that blows us all out of existence."

"That's reassuring," said Quentin. He drew a few stick figures running from the black hole.

"In the portal, you can navigate through ten different dimensions. Do you know any of them?"

Quentin put down the pen. "Well, you've got your height, and your length, and your width... and time. I like maps, you see." He drew a graph with an X axis for length, a Y axis for height, and a Z axis for width, and drew a cube around it for time.

"How fortunate." Dalton paused and smiled. He was beginning to like Quentin, whom he'd feared more than anything up until that point. "I'm going to send you in there. I want you to only focus on those four dimensions. Ignore the others. They will send you into bizarre alternate realities in which you might get lost forever."

"Sounds like rubbish," said Quentin. He redrew the different axes of his original map in a manner in which they appeared to be folding over one another. He added a dismembered stick figure floating inside it.

"Indeed. I sent Father Peter into the void with the chip I put into Clyde, so I should be somewhat capable of modifying the void from within, despite other forces working against me. I'm going to use the chip to determine the path you must take toward your destination in the space-time continuum."

"Shit, all right." Quentin drew a point in his graph and circled it.

"You'll need to use those mapping skills to find your way to those coordinates, because once you go through the void, I can no longer communicate with you."

"That sounds like somethin' I can do." Quentin polished up his drawing.

"Once you're in there, you must get to the coordinates the chip will have located. Of course, Father Peter won't be there; unlike you, he lost all contact with his virtual self and is now sparsely spread across the ten different dimensions."

"Poor priest." Quentin drew an arrow toward the dismembered stick figure's face and wrote, *Father Peter.*

"But once you're in there, your code form should help you keep your consciousness together and with a bit of luck, you might be able to find the location where I will be sending you."

"There's no need for luck," said Isidora, who stood behind the two of them. She pulled Brooke, the formerly large rat, out of her pocket. "Use her chip to help guide Quentin."

Dalton smiled widely at Isidora. "You found her. Excellent."

Quentin took Brooke out of Isidora's hands and petted her gently with two of his blistered fingers.

"Quentin, I will be sending you to my own apartment, just over a year ago." Dalton paused, feeling his throat close up in an attempt to get more words out. He closed his eyes, exhaled deeply and resumed his explanation.

"In there, you will find me trying to kill myself. You must talk me out of it. If you do, I won't create the afterlife and this whole sequence of events will have never happened, closing up the interdimensional portal at this point in space and time, allowing for all our lives to go back to normal. Can you do that?"

"Anythin' not to turn into a bloody demon. Let's map it out."

*   *   *

"The surface of the water in the middle of the Albert Dock was point 0. That's where the portal brings you," said Quentin, tracing the map he'd designed within the virtual afterlife, while Dalton coded next to him. He now drew on Karl's yellow legal notepad. Dalton couldn't concentrate with Quentin drawing on his desk.

"That means point 0 is also right here in the laboratory." Dalton pointed to the entry of the void.

"Right. Since point 0 is there, using the address of your apartment, we can easily locate where I have to go in the first three dimensions once I'm inside."

Dalton gave him his address. By juxtaposing a map of Liverpool against Quentin's map, they established the coordinates of Dalton's flat within the void.

"The trouble now is, when you're in the void, time stands still. It was a feature of the virtual afterlife I had programmed, thinking it would make it eternal. By reverse-engineering the standstill command, I just might be able to give time the vector necessary to send you back to the moment before my suicide attempt by cutting through the sixth dimension." Dalton typed code into the program, stopped, edited, and coded some more.

"Nearly there?" asked Isidora, looking around. Chief Constable Glasgow appeared to have vanished and Darcy was taking on all the demons herself as more and more poured out of the void.

"Don't pressure me," grumbled Dalton.

Stanley gawked at Quentin. His face was hardly recognizable from all the burns and blisters. The colour in his eyes had nearly faded away entirely. Though he never complained, his pain was visible; his pen trembled in his hand as he fought to draw out his maps. Stanley flicked open his switchblade and held it between Dalton's eyes.

"Mr. Scientist, which eye do you like best? If you don't hurry up, I'll cut it out!"

A bolt of electricity hit the knife, projecting it out of Stanley's hand and into the void.

"Children shouldn't play with knives!" Darcy shouted and went back to frying demons.

Stanley deftly reached into Quentin's pocket and extracted his switchblade. He stored it in his own pocket.

Dalton typed away some more, smiled, and hit one more key like a classical pianist finishing a virtuoso performance. He turned around as though he were awaiting applause. "There, I've done it. Go in there, and you'll travel through time and space back to my apartment."

"Brilliant!" said Isidora, staring at the screen in wonder.

"Hang on," said Quentin. "What about all the other dimensions?"

Dalton nodded. "About that. I don't quite have them figured out just yet."

"How long will it take for you to figure them out?" asked Isidora.

Dalton avoided her icy stare. He paused, leaned backed in his chair, away from his screen, and sighed. "Years, probably."

"Years?" Stanley exclaimed. "We probably don't have a bloody hour until Quentin goes full demon!"

Dalton adjusted his shirt collar, which felt increasingly tight. "I don't have control over those dimensions. I didn't intend for them to interfere with the afterlife; I only expected dimensions one through four to have any significance. Whoever hacked my system controls the other dimensions."

"God and Satan," said Isidora, in an oddly distant tone, staring into the void. "Those are their dimensions."

Dalton shrugged. "Call them whatever you like. It would take years for me to get through their insane firewalls."

"Hellfire," said Isidora.

"Whatever helps you understand it."

Darcy found herself surrounded by demons. She felt her abilities diminishing as her energy began to run low. She desperately needed a break to recover her strength, but the more exhausted she grew, the more demons appeared.

"Dalton, I can't fend them off much longer," she cried out.

"You know what? Fuck the other dimensions," said Quentin. "We've got the time, and the location. That's all we need for me to get there, right?"

Dalton nodded. "In theory, yes. I simply cannot anticipate how the other dimensions might interfere with what I've programmed."

"I'll just ignore them," said Quentin.

Dalton grimaced, then tried to give Quentin a reassuring smile, but his face contorted awkwardly. "Right. Well. We don't have much of a choice." He pointed to Brooke, who was in Quentin's pocket. "Can you please give her to me? I have to get the chip out."

Quentin turned away from Dalton and covered Brooke with his hand. "No."

"You cannot possibly be serious."

"I'd like to bring her with me."

Dalton shook his head. "She's likely lost touch with her virtual self. Bring her in there with you and she'll burst into an infinite number of pieces throughout time and space."

"I bet you she hasn't. She probably hated when Father Peter made her small and turned her into an angel-rat or whatever. She wants to be big again. Just like me, she's latched onto her virtual self."

"Quentin, leave the bloody rat behind!" exclaimed Isidora.

Dalton turned back to his computer and scrolled through some code. "Oh. You're right. Her program is still active." He typed a few lines of code. "I've made her your tour guide. When you get in there, follow her. She's processed all the data from your map, she will know where to go better than you do because she won't be distracted by her own perception of reality. I have a lot more control over the rats than I do over you."

"Why?" asked Stanley.

"Because humans deserve free will. Ethically, it would be unthinkable to use my program to control you. The rats were programmed to expand the afterlife for me thanks to those chips. Since Clyde's program vanished after whatever Father Peter did to the rats, I could only use the chip to collect data when Father Peter brought it back into the void. With Brooke, I will still be able to use her to navigate through the void since, for some reason, she's still part virtual."

"I told you, it's because she wants to be big again," Quentin said, patting the rat on the head.

"Funny how that works," said Isidora. "By giving us so much free will and power over our environment, you made it possible for Father Peter to denature it entirely, allowing for the other dimensions to interfere with it."

"You're right," said Dalton. "I couldn't give you that much freedom and expect to maintain control over the situation."

"You can't be a prisoner in your own mind, so if your mind dictates your environment, expect the walls to fall," said Quentin. "Now do I go in there or not?"

Dalton pressed the "enter" key on his keyboard and turned to Quentin. "Whenever you're ready."

"Preferably sooner than later, but no pressure, love," said Darcy, as she shocked a demon biting her hand.

Quentin nodded and approached the void. "All right, I'm off, then. Catch you later. Or earlier, I suppose." He waved to the others and stepped toward the void.

"Wait!" said Isidora.

Quentin turned around.

"There's something I need to tell you." Her voice quivered.

A long pause followed, and Isidora became increasingly aware that everyone had stopped whatever they were doing and were now staring at her. Even the demons had stopped fighting Darcy, waiting to hear what Isidora had to say.

"G'wed, then," said Quentin.

She hesitated. "Have fun in there!" Quentin's eyebrows raised slightly, and Isidora felt her cheeks burn hotter than when she was in demon form. "But not too much fun, of course. We wouldn't want you getting lost in some hole in time and space for all eternity." She giggled, then suddenly became very aware of the fact that she didn't know what to do with her arms. She shifted from one position to another self-consciously. "In fact, don't have fun. I hope you hate it in there."

Isidora tried to take a step forward for one final embrace in an attempt to distract him from what she'd said, but she tripped over her own feet and nearly fell to the ground, saving herself with a few stabilizing hops.

Quentin furrowed his brow but smiled. "Thank you."

He stepped into the void and vanished.

Dalton broke the oppressively awkward silence that followed. "This evening, my virtual afterlife was hacked by the heavens, I witnessed some of the most brutal deaths imaginable, I got possessed by an old man, I murdered my own sister, the Pope stormed my laboratory and tried to start the apocalypse, and I watched my demonic ex-boyfriend vanish from existence. But that, Isidora... What you just did right there... That was the most horrific scene of all."

Stanley gave Dalton a high-five.

CHAPTER FOURTEEN

Quentin surveyed the void. His map illuminated the X, Y and Z axes in the darkness. He looked to his side. Brooke stood by him, big again.

"Right. It worked. The mad scientist did it."

Brooke said nothing. She darted in the direction of the vector Dalton had programmed, leading the way toward Dalton's apartment on the level of the first three dimensions.

"This seems to be workin', wouldn't you say? I'm guessin' at some point we'll hit a sort of wall or somethin' where we can travel through time... What was it he said? By cuttin' through the sixth dimension? He's probably set somethin' up so I know where to find that, right? You're supposed to know, he put all that information inside of you."

Brooke carried on ahead, ignoring Quentin. He scanned his surroundings. There was still nothing but grids defining the measurements of the first three dimensions, until a shadowy figure walking toward him appeared.

"Hey, Brooke, do you see that? Who the bloody hell is that?"

Brooke did not stop moving, leaving Quentin no choice but to follow her and continue walking toward the figure ahead. As he got closer, he noticed an animal walking just ahead of the figure.

It was Brooke.

He looked at his own rat. Brooke was running straight toward herself. He looked up and the figure's features gradually became visible.

It was himself.

Only much more proper. He was radiant, his nose was straight like it had never been broken, he didn't have any tattoos, his eyes sparkled, and he certainly wasn't transitioning toward a demonic state. He wore a bowler hat and a light grey trench coat over a suit and tie. Proper Quentin smiled at Quentin and nodded to him in a greeting manner.

"A fine day to go out and walk your rat, wouldn't you say?" said Proper Quentin, tipping his hat as he passed.

"Who the bloody hell do you think you are?" asked Quentin, but Proper Quentin carried along in the other direction.

Quentin looked back at Brooke. Unphased by the encounter, she continued on forward toward wherever Dalton had commanded her to go.

They crossed another figure, also led by a rat resembling Brooke, but its eyes glowed red. As they got closer, Quentin noticed that the other man was yet again himself, but in total demon form. His eyes were completely black, his skin burned red, and it crumbled away into ash with every movement he made.

"What the bloody hell is that?" Quentin said.

"Keep starin' at me like that and I'll cut yer throat," Demon Quentin hissed. Quentin looked away and they walked past one another. Brooke carried on ahead.

As Quentin followed Brooke, he observed various familiar figures walking past him and across from him. A Heavenly Karl wished him "Good day" and a hellish Pope Clement XV called out "Death to the English!" and whacked Quentin with his staff. Darcy, wearing a black wedding dress, ran up to Quentin and slapped him across the face. She demanded to know where her groom went and ran off. Shortly after, Father Peter, wearing an entirely white tuxedo, walked up to Quentin, gave him a hug and thanked him for covering for him.

Quentin looked down and was alarmed by what he saw. Brooke had multiplied into three Brookes, then seven, then more than a dozen Brookes. They started running off in different directions.

"Wait, which one of you is the real one? Who do I follow?"

Some of the Brookes began running up and down the Y axis while others spiralled about the X or Z axes. Some walked up strange angles resembling the line of an exponential function, while others mirrored this motion the opposite direction in a logarithmic manner. Quentin tried to follow one Brooke, and then another, only to find himself completely lost. He stopped and sat down, suspended upside down on a slight angle relative to his original position.

"Fuck."

*   *   *

"Fuck," said Dalton, looking at the screen.

"What is it?" asked Isidora.

"The fifth dimension began to interfere with him, but he got past it by following Brooke. I needed her to guide him to the loophole in the sixth dimension I created, allowing him to travel through the fourth. I think he's lost somewhere between the fifth and the sixth dimensions right now."

"What the fuck does any of that mean?" asked Stanley, reaching into his pocket for Quentin's switchblade. Isidora gave him a stern look and shook her head. He scowled but released the knife.

"In the fifth dimension, you can find a world slightly different from ours, with the same initial starting point, that is, the Big Bang. In the sixth, you can see a plane of possible worlds with the same starting point as ours, at different points in time."

"Whoa," said Stanley, picturing himself in the Palace of Versailles living like King Louis XIV of France.

"I commanded Brooke to find the time vector I programmed, which would cut through the sixth dimension to bring Quentin back in time to find me in my flat. But he's just floating around in there."

"Can't you use Brooke?" asked Isidora. "Can't you do something to her to get Quentin back on the right path?"

Dalton paused, staring at the screen. "The trouble is, I'm not entirely sure which Brooke is the real one."

"What does that mean?" asked Stanley.

"Whoever hacked my computer doesn't want Quentin to get to where I need him to go. And they've managed to duplicate Brooke an infinite number of times. It will take me ages to locate the right Brooke."

"Wouldn't she be the only one to respond to your command?" asked Isidora.

Dalton pursed his lips. "Respectfully, Isidora, you haven't the slightest clue what you're talking about, so please keep your ideas to yourself." He paused and exhaled heavily. He regretted how he'd spoken to her; she was one of the few people he actually liked. She was rational and hardly ever smiled. When she did, it was only halfway. "I apologize for my tone. You see, the hackers, they've... I've lost control entirely."

*   *   *

"Hello, Quentin."

Still sitting in an unclear point in space and time, Quentin turned around. Dalton stood behind him. Quentin smiled.

"Oh, brilliant! How did you get in here?"

Quentin's smile faded slightly after getting a better look at Dalton. His jerky movements and shining eyes gave him an almost metallic appearance. His features seemed almost too symmetrical to be natural, like a doll. It wasn't the real Dalton, nor was it a heavenly or demonic Dalton. He was artificial, yet transcendence emanated from his expression, which made Quentin feel deeply understood.

"I've always been here," Dalton said, raising his arms and looking around him. "Everyone and everything have always been here." His voice resonated as though he spoke into a tin can.

Quentin shook his head. "No, mate, I just got here. I know what you're tryin' to say, that there's no bloody time here so I couldn't have just gotten here or some rubbish like that, but I definitely just got here."

"Follow me."

Quentin didn't move but looked around. The grid of his map

slowly folded over and twisted in a bizarre manner.

"Stop fuckin' with me map."

Dalton smiled with his mouth but not his eyes. His image seemed to flicker occasionally. "You cannot map out what your mind won't let you see."

"No fuckin' shit."

"You cannot keep ignoring the other dimensions around you. There is no reason to fear them. Countless opportunities lie before you, should you choose to open your mind."

"Actually, I'm really just lookin' for me rat..."

Dalton looked to his side. A luminous crack had formed in the void. It grew wider and wider, until it absorbed the void all together. Quentin felt warm humidity fill the area and a bug buzzed right by his ear. He waved it away. Around him appeared a green and wild tropical environment. Quentin looked up.

"Mate, why's your sister climbin' a coconut tree?"

"Fuck, wrong world, hang on."

Dalton snapped his fingers. Dalton and Quentin stood in a room together. It was the warehouse from the afterlife that Quentin had turned into Buckingham Palace. Isidora sat at the piano and played a joyful Beethoven sonata.

"It's what you wanted," said Dalton. "Eternity in the virtual afterlife."

"I'm just lookin' for me rat."

"You have the greatest opportunity ever known to man. Of all the world's possibilities, here you are, in the midst of it all, capable of choosing which path to go down. Why follow a rat to where someone else is telling you to go, when you can live in whichever world you so choose?"

Quentin shook his head. "It's not real."

"What is real? What isn't? How is this universe more real than the one your conscious mind was born into, without any choice in the matter? You have absolute freedom, Quentin. Why insist on remaining a prisoner? Let yourself be free. Do whatever you want."

Isidora finished playing her piece and turned around, waiting for a reaction.

"It's not real," said Quentin.

"What's not real?" asked Isidora with a laugh. "It's a real piano, Quentin. Come over and have a look."

Quentin walked over to the piano and pressed down on a couple keys. A perfect fifth.

"I suppose it seems real. But I remember this part. The old man will be here soon."

"What old man?" asked Isidora.

"You know... the unclean one."

Isidora laughed and kissed Quentin on the cheek.

"I don't get you sometimes, but you always know how to make me smile."

Stanley ran into the room.

"Daddy!" he exclaimed and threw his arms around Quentin's waist.

"What the fuck?" Quentin said to Dalton, pushing Stanley away.

"You have an infinite number of possibilities before you and an infinite number of outcomes. Why not choose the one you like best?" said Dalton.

"If you think this bloody nightmare is what I'd want, you're mad," said Quentin, eyeing the affectionate Stanley and doting Isidora in disgust. He missed his stand-offish Izzy and her half-smiles and the Stan who loved beer and switchblades. "I enjoyed my life. Just as it was."

"Are you sure about that?" Dalton asked. He snapped his fingers and the two were now in a pub in Liverpool, sitting on bar stools. Quentin felt tired, angry, and dizzy. He was drunk. An empty bottle stood in front of him.

"Mate, I'll fuckin' kill you," said a raspy voice next to Quentin.

Quentin looked at Dalton. He stared straight ahead, drinking sparkling water. "You think this is funny?" Quentin asked Dalton.

The man with the raspy voice grabbed Quentin by the shirt collar and shook him aggressively. "You hear me? I'll fuckin' kill you for what you did."

Quentin felt compelled to repeat the words he'd once spoken to that same man, at that same establishment. He smirked. "I'm not the married one. I did nothing wrong, she did."

"I swear, I'll do it. I'll kill you."

Quentin looked at his best mate. Still holding Quentin's shirt collar, his eyes were wide open and filled with tears, his brows were furrowed, his teeth were clenched, and his breathing was erratic.

"G'wed. Try," Quentin challenged.

The man slammed Quentin against the edge of the bar. His nose was crushed and he felt himself inadvertently bite straight through his own lip. He grabbed the empty beer bottle in front of him. The man pulled him back up with the intention of slamming him against the bar once more, but Quentin broke the bottle on the edge of the counter and cut the man's throat. The man clasped his hands against his own throat, but it did not prevent the blood from spraying out of him in every direction. He fell off the stool, and while panic and chaos broke out in the bar, Quentin watched the man die, mildly irritated by the throbbing pain in his nose and lip.

"You enjoyed your life, just as it was, you say?" said Dalton, still staring straight ahead, sipping his sparkling water. The sound of sirens approached, and Dalton pointed at the pub's front door, without shifting his blank gaze. "I think this is the part where they arrest you."

Quentin sprang around and faced Dalton. "Fuck off. None of this is real. Where's me rat?"

You still feel no remorse, do you, murderer? said an authoritative voice inside Quentin's mind. *You truly have the perfect mind. Now, get out of this little dreamland. Reality is much greater than it appears to be now.*

"How do I get out?" Quentin asked the voice.

Dalton dropped his glass of water, stiffly snapped his head to the side and stared at Quentin. His shining, unblinking eyes somehow communicated a sense of urgency despite being emotionless. "Ignore him," said Dalton. "It's a trap. Don't listen to him. You could have it all, any world you like, if you just stay with me. Beyond these worlds, the laws of physics as you know them will fall apart."

Kill the scientist to break free of the sixth dimension and see what the world truly could be.

Policemen burst into the bar, coming to arrest him. Quentin didn't trust the voice inside his head, but he didn't trust Dalton either. He looked at the bloody, broken bottle in his hand, and looked back at Dalton. He fixed his grip on the weapon and hesitantly raised it. Dalton shook his head.

You killed once. You can kill again.

Quentin sliced open Dalton's throat. With that motion, he created another crack in reality, and darkness streamed through. The crack grew ever more, taking over the sixth dimension.

*   *   *

"He went straight past it," said Dalton, sitting at the computer.

"Straight past what?" asked Stanley.

"Straight past the sixth dimension. I can't believe it," said Dalton.

"What does that mean?" asked Isidora.

"It means he went right past where he was supposed to go to get back in time."

"Where did he go instead?" asked Stanley.

"He's accelerating through the seventh, eighth and ninth dimensions, discovering a plane of different possible universes."

"How is that different from where he was before?" asked Isidora.

"The starting point of these worlds isn't necessarily the Big Bang. They evolved in the most extraordinary ways and are subject to entirely different laws of physics than those which govern the known universe."

"Can he fly?" asked Stanley.

"Perhaps," said Dalton.

Meanwhile, Darcy struggled to hold back an exponentially greater number of demons, who were now beginning to flood the laboratory.

"Whatever he's doing in there, it's making me job quite difficult," said Darcy.

Dalton looked at the interdimensional portal. It had grown substantially in size, taking over nearly half the laboratory.

"The other dimensions are beginning to flood the known

universe," said Dalton.

"The gates of Hell are opening," said Isidora.

"Whatever helps you understand it," said Dalton. "In sum, the world is about to end."

*   *   *

Quentin was in an endless free fall, spiralling through an infinite loop of smoke and flames. His lungs filled with acid, and collapsed, releasing the corrosive fluid which burned everything within him. He felt as though a swarm of wasps was continuously stinging him all over his body. Amidst the blinding and deafening agony, he struggled to grasp at anything that reminded him of the humanity he once had.

Open your eyes, the voice in his mind commanded. At once, Quentin obeyed, and the surrounding air stung them.

Do you see the doom in which He forces us to suffer? Endless fire, endless torture. Suffer in vain for the lie of salvation; fail to be saved and suffer forever.

Quentin did his best to respond to the voice in his mind, despite the pain clouding his reason.

"None of this is real. It's not that simple. Look, I'm just lookin' for me rat. She's quite big for a rat. Have you seen her?"

A thunderous cackle filled Quentin's mind. *Why do you still fight me, Quentin? I am not your enemy. The enemy is the one who has damned you.*

"If this is Hell, I'm pretty sure it's me bloody sins or whatever that got me here, so I suppose me worst enemy is me'self."

That's His lie. He fills you with desires and impulses, asks you to torture yourself your whole life to deny them despite your inevitable failure, and then damns you here to punish you for your failings.

"What a bloody wanker. So, me rat. Where is she?"

Quentin, you must let go of the world you thought you knew. Join us in our revolution and the world will be free. Free of torture, free of suffering. Free of God's merciless cruelty.

The more Quentin opposed the voice in his mind, the more he

felt the acid within him, and the fire blazing around him, fade away.

"I don't know, mate. It sounds like you're asking me to suffer, with a promise of salvation in the end. I don't bloody buy it. I'll ask you this one more time. Where is me bloody rat?"

*   *   *

"There has to be a solution," said Isidora, pacing around, through the growing number of demons filling the laboratory. "Quentin has to go back to the past so that we all forget the last thing I said to him. It's far too humiliating."

"It's not that bad for you," protested Stanley. "You're God's Paladin. You can do whatever you like in the end, side with God, or the Devil, and no matter who wins the war you get all the glory for being the Paladin. It's rubbish for us because we have to choose sides and if our side loses, we vanish from existence."

Stanley spread his hand on Dalton's desk, flicked open Quentin's switchblade, and repeatedly brought the knife down onto the desk between each of his fingers, each time, faster and faster.

"Stop that," said Dalton.

"Don't worry, I've done this plenty of times. I won't cut me'self."

"I don't care about that. My desk. You're wrecking it."

Stanley stabbed Dalton's hand. Dalton inhaled sharply, trying not to scream from the pain.

"Why would you do that? I'm trying to save the world!" said Dalton.

"You said you didn't care if I got cut. Very rude."

Dalton wiped some blood off his hand, shook his head and resumed coding with his good hand.

"I can't do this anymore," said Darcy.

Countless demons held back both her arms, stopping her from fighting. They clawed at her, bit her, and burned her.

"Isidora, do something!" said Stanley.

"I'm not supposed to," she said. "That's not my role. There are rules, and I have to respect them."

"For Christ's sake, auntie!" cried Stanley.

"Exactly!" said Darcy, her voice muffled by the demons piling up on her.

"I never listen to rules," said Stanley. "Sometimes I get away with it, sometimes I get scolded. But either way, I get to do what I want. Everythin' is much better that way because I have loads more fun."

"And look where that got you," said Dalton.

Stanley nodded, oblivious to the evident sarcasm in Dalton's voice. "I have cool friends, beer, ciggies, knives, whatever I want. Just do what you want, auntie."

Isidora reached into her pocket and pulled out a pack of cigarettes. She lit one, took a deep, smoke-filled breath, which cleared her head. She exhaled, and the buzz relaxed her into disobedience.

"You know what? You're right. Fuck it."

Isidora flicked on her lighter. The fire shone a glorious, divine blue. She stepped into a mass of demons and set them on fire as she made her way over to Darcy. Racing around frantically, bumping into one another, the demons set fire to each other. Isidora kicked away the demons heaped on Darcy, extended her hand, pulled Darcy up and wiped off the green, sulphurous demon bile that covered her face with her sleeve.

"Excuse me," said a small demon, tugging at Isidora's shirt from behind. "That wasn't fair."

"Life is unfair. Why would death be any different?" Isidora extinguished her cigarette butt on the small demon's head and it vanished into a pile of ash. She lit another cigarette.

Dalton cleared his throat. "I have an idea about how to get Quentin back on the right track. But it's risky."

Isidora rushed back to Dalton.

"Whatever it is, it's worth trying," said Isidora. "What can you do?"

Dalton pointed to the screen as if Isidora and Stanley were capable of understanding the code it displayed.

"At this rate, he will soon be in the tenth dimension: the point where everything imaginable will be before him. Worlds like ours, similar to ours, or entirely unlike ours, will all be within his reach."

"My God," said Isidora.

"Exactly," said Darcy.

"Whatever helps you understand it," Dalton added. "Remember the passage I created through the sixth dimension?"

"To travel in time!" exclaimed Stanley.

"Correct. I believe I could render it visible from the tenth, since all possible universes are within his reach from there."

"It sounds a little... overwhelming," said Isidora. "And with that many possibilities before him, what are the odds he happens upon the right one?"

"Have you ever gone into an overwhelmingly large store for only one very specific purchase? You go straight in and straight out, and you don't even notice all the other rubbish around you. I'm hoping it has that effect."

"I have no idea what you're talking about. I get distracted by everything," said Isidora.

"Luckily, Quentin is a man," said Dalton.

Darcy shot a divine bolt at her brother's shoulder, stunning him.

"That was a terribly sexist thing to say. And last time we went shopping together you were the one who got distracted by all the rubbish."

Dalton rubbed his shoulder. "Excuse me, Darcy, but that was at a comic book convention, and the merchandise was brilliant; it was the complete opposite of rubbish. Very different situation."

Dalton turned to Isidora. "I got an exact replica of the Third Doctor's sonic screwdriver."

Isidora smoked, resisted the urge to insult him for his irrelevance and changed the subject. "You really think that having all the different universes imaginable before you wouldn't be distracting?"

"Well, the most likely scenario is that it's far too much for the human mind to handle and that Quentin just bursts into oblivion." Dalton gestured an explosion with his hands and winced in pain from the wound inflicted by Stanley.

Isidora took his injured hand.

Dalton shook his head. "I understand why you're attracted to me, but I'm not interested in women. However, if I were heterosexual, I am sure the attraction would be mutual."

"Shut up, you idiot." She passed her fingers over his wound and it healed. "Now, get back to work."

Dalton typed furiously with both hands.

CHAPTER FIFTEEN

Quentin had grown tired of falling through fire and looked around for a way out. There seemed to be nothing but smoke and flames. He grabbed around fruitlessly, seeking something to hold onto.

Abandon all hope, Quentin. This is where it ends.

"I don't believe that. You said yourself that reality is much greater than it appears. There's nothin' great about any of this."

Quentin remembered how he'd gotten out of the sixth dimension; by killing Dalton. The way to break out of this dimension would therefore be to kill the voice inside his head... unless he never really needed to *kill* Dalton. He just needed a way to stop his influence on him.

I see those dark thoughts of yours. Do not waste your time; I cannot be killed. I am your past, your present, and your future. I am everything, everywhere you turn, everywhere you go. I cannot be silenced.

Quentin listened closely to the words he heard. It then occurred to him; he *heard* those words. The voice wasn't in his mind at all. The source was external.

"Maybe I can't shut you up, but I can stop hearin' you."

Quentin shut his eyes, grabbed both his ears and tore them off. A blinding pain followed from the tearing of skin and cartilage, and a constant, high-pitched ringing replaced the voice. The feeling of falling stopped; he had the impression he was now levitating on thin air. He took a deep breath, and the purest air filled his lungs. All agony vanished in a flash and was replaced by a sense of relief. He opened his eyes and found himself surrounded by a white light. It filled the world around him, not in an overwhelming manner, but in a warm and comforting way.

In the midst of the white light appeared a pond, reflecting a warm shade of purple. He looked up. A purple sky had formed above him. He crawled toward the pond and looked at his reflection. It made him burst into laughter. He plunged his hands into the pond. The water felt thick as honey yet smooth as silk. He splashed his face with the water and felt the ecstasy of rejuvenation. He jumped inside the pond and found himself laying in a meadow full of poppy flowers, surrounded by large trees with luminous green leaves that twisted and turned in a fairy tale-like manner. He sat up and looked to his left. Edward Reid was in his car, parked under a tree.

"How was prison?" Edward asked from the window.

"Was all right, but I had to rip me ears off to get out." Quentin touched his ears and realized they were still there.

"You comin' in?" Edward waved him over.

Quentin walked over to the car and got inside. They drove to a deserted country road. To the east were rolling green hills, and to the west the Irish Sea.

"Where would you like to go?" Edward asked.

"Where can I go?"

"How about home?"

Quentin looked into the cup holder, where a can of beer sat. He took a swig and tossed it out the window. A gust of wind carried it all the way out to the sea, where it finally fell. It skipped a few times like a pebble and dropped like a bomb had gone off; a fountain of water shot several feet out of the sea.

"Where is home?"

"Wherever you want it to be."

Quentin looked toward the hills. Pope Clement XV was there, shearing sheep with Father Peter. The wool turned into snow, and the Pope's shear turned into a shovel. He handed it to Father Peter, who shovelled the snow to the side. The snow turned into a rocket ship. The Pope and Father Peter stepped inside, and it blasted off. It turned into a paper airplane and flew across the horizon.

"Did you see that?" asked Quentin.

"What do we see? What don't we see? How do we know if we really see what we see? I see the sea; what do you see?"

"Yeah, but I'm really just lookin' for me rat."

"There are plenty of rats in multiple worlds."

"I'm looking for one in particular." Quentin looked at the road ahead. Brooke was right in front of them.

"Stop the car!" yelled Quentin.

"I can't," replied Edward.

"What do you mean, you can't?"

"I'm not drivin' the car. I'm not doing anythin'." Edward lifted his hands off the steering wheel and laughed.

Quentin yanked the emergency brake, but they hit Brooke. She flew into the air, landed, and rolled along the road several feet ahead of them. The two stepped out of the car and approached the lifeless beast.

"Fuck, Eddie, that was me rat."

A bell rang behind them. "It's not dead, you know."

They turned around. There stood Stanley, getting off his bike. He walked over and joined them, still wearing his helmet.

"Looks pretty dead," said Edward.

"Oh, the rat's dead, sure." Stanley took off his helmet and pointed to his own head. "What's underneath isn't."

Stanley handed Quentin back his switchblade. Quentin opened Brooke's side and found the chip.

"It's useless when it's not in Brooke, though. She was guiding me with it."

The paper airplane flew toward the group and landed next to them.

"Sorry guys, that's mine." Father Peter came running up to them from the hills and picked up the plane. It turned into a pile of cocaine.

"Put the chip in there and snort it," Father Peter said, holding out his cocaine-filled hand.

"No fuckin' way. It was inside a rat a moment ago."

Quentin felt a gentle hand touch his shoulder. "Grow a pair and do it." He turned around. His eyes met Isidora's; she gave him a half-smile.

"Very well. I've probably snorted worse."

Father Peter put the cocaine onto the hood of the car and Quentin dropped the chip inside. He did a line, and then another, and another, until there wasn't anything left.

"You could have at least shared," grumbled Father Peter.

Quentin felt all-powerful. He grabbed Stanley's bicycle and hurled it into the Irish Sea with one hand; it spun around itself like a Frisbee. Quentin picked up the car and tossed it into the sea as well. It cut right through the surface of the water without creating the slightest ripple. But the sea faded away, as did the road, and the hills, and the people around him, into darkness... and code. Code everywhere. Quentin knew exactly where he had to go.

*   *   *

"I believe he took the chip out of Brooke and put it into himself," said Dalton.

"He should have done that in the first place," said Isidora.

"He likes his freedom," said Stanley.

Darcy waved to Isidora in an attempt to attract her attention. "Isidora, would you mind coming back over here? We have a bit of a problem."

She pointed to the interdimensional portal. It now filled the vast majority of the laboratory and was growing at an increasingly rapid rate.

"Let's hope he gets there soon," said Isidora.

"I'm afraid it might be too late," replied Darcy.

The portal expanded, taking over the entire laboratory. Dalton, Stanley, Isidora and Darcy vanished from existence.

*   *   *

Almost there. Keep going, Quentin told himself, nearing the passage through the sixth dimension. The code around him flickered a couple times. He continued toward the passage, and sections of code began to disappear and were replaced by the void.

Fuck off, not now, not when I'm this close. The code disappeared around him more and more rapidly, until there was nearly nothing left.

I'm not going to fuckin' make it. He threw himself forward helplessly in a final attempt to reach the passage, and in the last nanosecond before everything vanished, Quentin Campbell travelled through time.

CHAPTER SIXTEEN

Dalton McGovern could no longer bear the weight of it all. Everyone around him expected nothing short of excellence from him. Having the greatest scientific mind of a generation, however, is of little significance without the strength of character one needs to overcome adversity. And at the age of twenty-eight, the Oxford-educated computer scientist was now taking more of an interest in biology. Indeed, sitting on the kitchen floor of his Liverpool flat, he evaluated that a quick, clean cut, half an inch deep, into his forearm, down to his wrist, would do the trick. The greatest challenge would be to overcome the pain after the first incision and repeat the operation on the other arm. Best to start with his left arm then, as he was left-handed. He deemed he would have a greater chance of succeeding using his dominant hand, despite the injury.

Someone knocked on his door.

"Bugger off," he shouted.

Quentin Campbell was part-demon, part-virtual, and part-convict. Breaking and entering was the least of his concerns and burning down doors with his hands was a neat little skill his demon-side had developed. He stepped over the ash that was once Dalton's door and strode into the kitchen.

Still sitting on the floor, Dalton pushed himself back with his legs into a corner between the counter and the adjacent wall, away from the intruder. Quentin's face was full of blisters and his eyes were black. His arms and neck were covered in prison tattoos, and he seemed to flicker away from time to time, like a lagging image on a computer screen. Quentin put his hand in his pocket and took out his switchblade. He knelt down and held it against Dalton's neck.

"I suppose I could just kill you. Unlike you, I'd do it right, and your death would undo this whole mess you've created."

Dalton whimpered.

"What's the matter? I thought you wanted to die."

"I... what are you?"

"What am I? I'm your bloody creation. You did this to me. You, and your bloody ego."

"I don't know who you are or—"

"Shut it. Do you want to die or not?"

Dalton hesitated. The terror in his eyes drifted away and shock took its place. He looked Quentin in the eye. "I suppose I don't."

"If I leave this flat, will you try to kill yourself?"

"I don't know—"

Quentin slammed Dalton against the wall with his burning arm and pressed the knife up against Dalton's neck, cutting him on the surface of his skin. A tear fell from Dalton's eye.

"No, I won't. I don't want to die. Please don't kill me."

Quentin nodded and pulled back from Dalton. "I believe you. But if you change your mind and think of killing yourself again..." Quentin rapidly brought the knife down to Dalton's eye and stopped half an inch away. Dalton flinched and cowered. "I'll be back."

I've lost my mind, thought Dalton. *I'm hallucinating, I'm suicidal... I've completely lost touch with reality. I need help.*

Quentin looked down at himself; he was disappearing. He smiled at Dalton.

"Well done, mate! We've changed the course of the future!" Quentin Campbell vanished.

Dalton took his phone out of his pocket and called Darcy. She picked up, and he burst into tears.

"I'm not well. I'm not well at all."

"I know, love. I had a feeling. I'm on my way over, just hang on."

*   *   *

Dalton McGovern learned that a pill a day kept suicidal thoughts away. With all that silly emotional rubbish behind him, he was able to focus on his research. By the end of the year, he had made some impressive advances in the field of artificial limbs controlled by the human mind. His technology was ready to be tested, and in the event his experiment proved successful, he expected to make a fair bit of money selling the concept to bionics companies. He knew that Karl had a taste for luxury. He wondered if he could win him back once he struck it rich; little did he know, however, that Karl had been arrested in France.

Meanwhile, Isidora Prentice sat inside Quentin Campbell's flat after she'd listened to a Welsh construction worker's theory that an old man living there had kidnapped her nephew. Her hand shook slightly as she lit a cigarette after meeting the ghost who haunted the flat. She exhaled slowly and was finally able to wrap her mind around what she'd witnessed.

"What are you going to do about the ghost?" she asked.

"We're not really sure," said Quentin. "We tried everythin', even the church, but they said it wasn't a serious enough case to justify sending over an exorcist."

"That's unacceptable," said Isidora. "Give me their number. We're getting an exorcism."

*   *   *

The Pope sat in front of Father Peter in the Vatican's reading room.

"You have to go to Liverpool to perform an exorcism," said the Pope. "There is this... crazy lady... she keep yelling at everyone at the Vatican on the phone and sending angry emails demanding an exorcism and it is too annoying."

"Is there even a demon?" asked Father Peter, laughing at monks' drawings in ancient religious texts.

"There is a real demon, some old man, but no one is very possessed, he just sort of latch onto some murderer's neck."

"Then there's no need for an exorcism. Sounds like a waste of time." Father Peter inadvertently tore out a page of the ancient book in his hands, crumpled it, and threw it behind him. The Pope slammed the book shut.

"What you are doing now is wasting my time. This lady, she keep nag, nag, nagging, I am sick of her bullshit. Go to Liverpool and get rid of the old man."

*   *   *

Father Peter reluctantly performed the exorcism and made drinks for Isidora, Stanley, Quentin and Edward. He sat with them at the table.

"I suppose you're ready to get back to normal, play soccer with your friends at school," Father Peter said to Stanley.

"I can't play football. I limp like a bloody idiot. Look at me foot." Stanley took off his shoe and revealed that the better part of his left foot was missing.

"That explains the limp," said Isidora.

"He lost it in the car accident," Quentin said.

"You know," said Father Peter, "on my flight over here, I was just reading about an amazing experiment by one of the researchers over at the University of Liverpool. Apparently, he's found a way to design the best prosthetics to replace arms, legs, hands or feet. They respond to the brain's impulses exactly like a real body part would. I read they're about to start human trials. Maybe, Stanley, you'd be a good candidate."

Stanley signed up for the experiment.

ACKNOWLEDGEMENTS

Mom, thank you for being the only mother in history to encourage her daughter to drop out of law school and pursue creative writing. The jury is still out on whether this was sound advice, but I am certainly having fun.

Thank you to my creative writing professor at Concordia University, Josip Novakovich, for your guidance and insight, and for encouraging me to send my manuscript to agents and publishers. Your support gave me the confidence I needed to achieve my goal of becoming a published author. I would also like to thank my classmates at Concordia from ENGL-226 B, winter semester 2020, for your valuable feedback: Ben, Marija, Clea, Virginia, Kemba, Lena, Christopher, Katie, Desire, Apollo, Evelyne, Silvio, Natasha.

A huge thank you to my friends who responded in the affirmative to the awful question, "Will you read my unpublished manuscript and tell me if it's any good?" Kevin Paquette, Thomas Sabbagh, Samuel Lemire, you've probably already guessed what you're getting for Christmas...

Thank you to my favourite science fiction fan, Alex Corelli, for your constant love and support. I hope my pseudoscience doesn't make your engineering brain cringe too much.

Thank you to all those who were there for me throughout this little adventure: my friends Yulia Petrosyan, Edward Liu, Rahul Taggar, Simon-Pierre Savard-Tremblay, and Theo Zych; the "RDM" (you know who you are); my Papa whose hometown of Shawinigan I hope I have honoured; my sister Caroline, the only person who makes me feel tall—and her husband Michel, who reminds me that I certainly am not. To my nephew William, you will get your copy on your 18th birthday.

Thank you to my family in the North of England who welcomed me during a memorable trip and inspired the setting of this story. I look forward to returning!

And a special thank you to my publisher and editor, Catherine Fitzsimmons, for giving me this wonderful opportunity.

Natasha Tremblay is a Government Press Secretary by day and a satirical science fiction & fantasy writer by night. Originally from Québec, the twenty-four-year-old Torontonian has a degree in English Literature from Concordia University and a certificate in Law from Université Laval. Tremblay claims that her main literary influences are Douglas Adams, Neil Gaiman and Stephen King. However, her mother believes that overexposure to *SpongeBob SquarePants*, *Futurama*, *South Park* and *Family Guy* in her formative years is to blame for her irreverent sense of humour.